"I'd li[...]
he whispered

He pressed her against the wall, then added teasingly, "Standing right here. . . ."

Her eyebrows rose. "Oh, yeah?" The idea excited her.

"Both of us fully clothed . . . or almost." He began to pull her long skirt up so it bunched at the meeting of their hips.

"And how do you propose to accomplish this feat?" Her fingers were moving up and down his ribs.

"I won't—" he laughed, jerking back "—if you keep that up."

"Ross Hammond, you're ticklish."

"Not in the least," he lied, but when she again wiggled her fingers, he pulled completely away from her, letting her skirt fall back to her ankles.

Even though she was tormenting him, she still wanted him. And though it was fun to know a wiggle of her finger could put him at arm's length, she preferred him closer. "Come here," she cajoled, her voice pitched low. Slowly she lifted her skirt. . . .

Maris Soule set *Storybook Hero*, her seventh Temptation, in the Sierra gold country of northern California. "I absolutely love that part of California, and when I make my first million, I plan to move there," she says. Maris also loves her heroine's unique career. "The more I learned about dolls and doll collecting, the more fascinated I became with the subject." We know you, too, will find much to love about this heartwarming tale of Sasha and her storybook hero, Ross.

Maris and her husband live with their two children in Fulton, Michigan.

Books by Maris Soule

HARLEQUIN TEMPTATION

Don't miss any of our special offers. Write to us at the following address for information on our newest releases.

Harlequin Reader Service
901 Fuhrmann Blvd., P.O. Box 1397, Buffalo, NY 14240
Canadian address: P.O. Box 603,
Fort Erie, Ont. L2A 5X3

Storybook Hero
MARIS SOULE

Harlequin Books

TORONTO • NEW YORK • LONDON
AMSTERDAM • PARIS • SYDNEY • HAMBURG
STOCKHOLM • ATHENS • TOKYO • MILAN

Dedicated to Elizabeth Costa

Published March 1989

ISBN 0-373-25342-7

1

"SHE'S DIFFERENT, MISTER. A real oddball, if you know what I mean. But your little girl would love her. All kids love the Doll Lady."

The waitress's words caused Ross Hammond to look across the booth at his daughter. In spite of having been released from the hospital over a month ago, Jenny Hammond was scarred, pale and still very frail. Silently the four-year-old fussed with an eighteen-inch old-fashioned cloth doll, seemingly oblivious to the conversation going on between her father and the waitress.

"Does everyone call her the Doll Lady?" asked Ross. The realtor and mail carrier had already mentioned the woman. Simply the sight of his daughter's doll seemed to trigger the subject.

"Most everyone. Her name's Sasha Peters, but she don't mind being called the Doll Lady. She loves dolls. That's one of hers." The waitress pointed a long red fingernail at Jenny's doll.

Ross doubted the doll had come from this small mountain town. It was a My Friends doll, a handmade original that his sister had bought in Sacramento—a spur-of-the-moment decision he'd blessed her for several times since. The doll had marked the turning point in Jenny's recovery.

For days after the car crash he'd feared he was going to lose his daughter. He couldn't understand it, but Jenny hadn't seemed to have the will to live. Then his sister had made that fateful stop at the hospital's gift shop. And from the moment Jenny saw the eighteen-inch fabric doll, life had come back into her eyes. The doll became her constant companion. And later, weeks later, they'd used the doll to persuade Jenny to do the physical therapy necessary to walk again; first the therapist would flex and stretch Anna's cloth legs, then she would do the same with Jenny's.

Looking more closely at the doll's face, the waitress nodded. "Yep, that's one of the Doll Lady's. I've seen a few copies, but what tells 'em apart is the eyes. Hers is always so real lookin'. Also, I'll bet you that doll has a navel and dimples in her cheeks . . . just like me."

Turning slightly, her hindside coming closer to Ross, the woman suggestively patted her fanny, then looked back at him and winked.

He knew she was flirting with him. She had been since Jenny and he had entered the nearly empty coffee shop. She'd given him a warm smile when she brought their menus and water, and had stood uncomfortably close when she took his order, almost overwhelming him with the strong aroma of her fragrance. After bringing their food she left for a while, then returned to stand by his side, conversing about the mild spring weather and again about Jenny's doll and the Doll Lady.

He wasn't interested in the waitress, but what she'd said about Jenny's doll fascinated him. Anna *did* have dimples on her bottom. He'd seen them the time Jenny spilled a glass of milk, right after the cast was taken off her arm, when her muscles were still weak. The milk had gone everywhere—through the sheet, Jenny's pj's and Anna's clothes. After the mess was cleaned up, he'd had to wash the doll. Under the old-fashioned blue gingham dress, long muslin petticoat and lace-trimmed cotton panties, he'd found two dimples stitched into the doll's bottom. The little detail had amused him.

"I hear your wife died in a car accident," the waitress went on, facing him again. "Must be mighty hard on you, losin' her and havin' to raise your kid by yourself. If you ever need any help . . . ah, you know, ah . . . adult companionship, I'm ah . . . around."

Ross looked down at his food. Word certainly did travel fast in this community. He'd bet it was the realtor who'd passed on the story about the crash. She'd been a talkative one, and so curious about why he was moving from Sacramento to Putnam.

Well, though he wasn't mourning Donna's death, neither was he interested in the waitress's offer. But rather than openly refuse the woman, he changed the subject. "Tell me more about the Doll Lady."

The waitress frowned. She knew he'd rejected her proposition. Taking a step back, she began to move away. "Nothin' more to tell. Sasha Peters makes dolls, lots of 'em, and goes around wearin' long dresses and bonnets. Personally, I think she's crazy, but kids like her. She holds a story hour every Wednesday mornin' at the library. You need anythin' else?"

"No, thanks."

The Doll Lady. Ross could picture an old, gray-haired lady in a long dress and bonnet—probably a little eccentric—telling stories to a group of children. Yes, Jenny might enjoy it.

Two weeks passed before Ross found the time to take his daughter to the Doll Lady's story hour. He'd thought it had taken forever to pack everything and clean out the house in Sacramento. It was taking forever plus to unpack and organize everything in the house he'd bought in Putnam.

Putnam, California. Altitude just under 3,000 feet, population 1,020—now 1,022. Not exactly a booming metropolis. His law partners had been dumbfounded when he announced he was moving here. "But why?" they'd all asked.

He couldn't really explain why—not to them, not to his parents, his sister or his friends. How did a man in his thirties, a man known by friends, associates and clients as a workaholic, explain a need to find himself?

He'd remembered Putnam from his teens. For three years in a row his uncle had brought him up here to go deer hunting. Each of those years he'd left Sacramento and his parents with a promise to bring home a trophy buck. But he never did. What he did bring back were memories—wonderful memories of days spent seeing nature at its finest; man-to-man camaraderie; a town that was friendly and a pace of life that was slow and relaxed.

In the late 1800s Putnam had been a bustling gold town and for a few short years had boasted a population of ten thousand, with miners working every foot of ground within a five-mile radius. But then the gold had petered out. Now Putnam depended on lumbering and tourism for its income. Summers were mild, although the temperature occasionally rose to ninety, and the winters were tolerable; the snow measured in inches rather than feet, as it was higher up in the Sierra Nevadas.

In all the years that had passed, Ross had never forgotten the area. When he'd needed to mentally escape the stress of his work, he'd remembered the wonderful smell of woodsmoke and pine, how the sunlight had streamed through the evergreens like rays of gold, the delightful sounds of the crickets at night and the daytime scolding of the blue jays.

His partners, friends and family hadn't understood his need to move to Putnam, had said he was crazy, but he knew he wasn't. Buying the old two-story wood-frame house just off the town's main street was the sanest thing he'd ever done. Maybe he'd never again be considered a success, but he'd find enough work to keep his mind active. As soon as Jenny and he were settled in, he planned to start remodeling the front two rooms of the house. That would be his office. He'd already gotten the necessary license and permits. The town of Putnam was going to have a lawyer. Not a supercharged overzealous business lawyer, but a laid-back homebody family lawyer. And he was going to be a family man, albeit that of a one-parent family.

In the six months since the accident he'd discovered how much a man could grow to love a little daughter. Jenny had become the center of his life, and he enjoyed every minute spent with her; nevertheless, he also knew she needed the companionship of other children. The Doll Lady's story hour would be the perfect way to introduce her to others her own age. When the next Wednesday came around, he made certain he kept the morning free.

"We're going to go hear a story," he announced, kneeling in front of Jenny to help her put on her gray wool coat. "There's a nice old lady at the library who has dolls and likes to tell stories to little boys and girls."

Jenny said nothing, her wide blue eyes gazing into his face.

"I'll be there with you," he promised. "Daddy won't leave you."

He wondered if she believed him. Up until the accident he'd certainly given her little reason to trust his word. He hated to think of the number of times he'd told her he'd be home before she went to bed, then wasn't. Donna had told him not to make promises he couldn't keep. The thing was, he'd always meant to be there. It was just that something—work—had always delayed him.

As they walked the two blocks to the library, Jenny's soft brown curls bounced above her collar with each step she took, and the cool spring air brought a touch of color to her pale cheeks. Ross held her hand; she clutched his fingers. In her other arm she held her doll. Anna went everywhere with them.

He knew Jenny was scared, so he talked to her along the way, pointing out the patches of snow that were still nestled in the shadow of the juniper bushes, the crocuses and daffodils just starting to break through the ground, and the new leaves beginning to appear on the willow trees that grew near the banks of the Yuba River where it cut through town. Jenny said nothing.

They walked by old brick and stone buildings decorated with picturesque iron doors and shutters. And they passed multigabled frame houses, whose many windows, like eyes, seemed to be watching them. His boots made a thudding sound on the worn wooden sidewalk, some of whose planks dated back over a hundred years. Jenny tried not to step on the cracks between the boards.

At the library, Ross pushed open a heavy wooden door and waited for his daughter to step inside. She hesitated, standing beside him, silently peering in at the rows and rows of shelving and books, her fingers never loosening their grip on his. "I won't leave you," he repeated softly. Without a word she entered the building.

Before he even had a chance to ask where the story hour was being held, the older woman seated behind an imposing oak desk pointed toward a side room. Ross guided his little daughter in that direction.

A young woman wearing a long-sleeved muted-blue wool dress was seated on a braided rug, two cardboard boxes by her side and a dozen preschoolers grouped in front of her. A book was open on her lap, but she wasn't reading from it. At the moment she was asking a little boy a question, and the other children were looking at him, either waiting for his answer, or waving their hands in the air to show they knew. Jenny tightened her grip, pressing herself even closer to Ross's leg.

Five women—mothers, Ross assumed—were also in the room. Two leaned against the shelves of books that lined the walls, and three sat on heavy wooden chairs. He edged up to the nearest standing one and whispered, "Couldn't the Doll Lady come today?"

The three seated women turned to look up at him, their expressions a combination of amusement and curiosity. He was still a new face in town. The mother he'd asked smiled, then nodded toward the woman seated on the braided rug. "That *is* the Doll Lady."

"That's her?"

Ross stared. Sasha Peters was not what he'd expected. Not at all. For one thing, she wasn't old. At the most he'd say she was in her late twenties. Nor did she have a gray hair on her head, although the tight, sassy curls that haloed her face were almost flaxen in color. And finally, she was beautiful. It was the only word he could think of to describe her. *Beautiful.*

Her features were delicate—almost like a porcelain doll's—her coloring a smooth peaches-and-cream. In many ways Sasha Peters reminded him of the storybook dolls his sister had once collected—except none of his sister's dolls had had the Junoesque figure he was looking at now. Below the Peter Pan collar of her blue wool dress, the Doll Lady's figure became outright voluptuous, the fullness of her breasts even more dramatic when compared to her narrow waist and trim hips.

Realizing he was staring, Ross quickly looked away— at a shelf of books. Ogling a woman's chest wasn't like him. Besides the fact that for years he'd been too busy with his work for more than a passing interest in a woman's bustline, he'd always been a leg man.

When he looked back, eyes as green as new leaves in spring met his.

FROM THE MOMENT he'd entered the room, the little child clinging to his hand, Sasha was acutely aware of Ross Hammond. His presence was like electricity in the air, a spark that brought her senses to life. Even as three-year-old Toby Reynolds, who usually said little, announced he was getting a baby sister or brother for Halloween, her ears caught the smooth, low timbre of Ross's whispered question. He was asking about her.

Sasha congratulated Toby, saying he must be very excited, and tried to concentrate on the children. But it wasn't easy. She could feel his gaze traveling over her, could sense when those eyes focused on her breasts.

Ever since she'd reached puberty and had jumped from a training bra to a size D cup within a single month, men had had a fixation for that part of her anatomy. At first she'd been embarrassed; then, when she was older, it had irritated her. Now she refused to let herself get angry; still, she didn't have much respect for men who couldn't see beyond her chest.

"Who wants a baby sister or brother? I'd rather have a kitten," stated outspoken four-year-old Mandy Miller.

"Kittens are nice, too," Sasha answered automatically. She looked away from the children at Ross. To her surprise, he was staring at a row of books, not at her breasts. Then he glanced back, and eyes as blue as sapphires met hers.

She knew who he was; in Putnam, newcomers were always talked about. For the past two weeks everywhere she'd gone she'd heard about Ross Hammond, the good-looking lawyer from Sacramento, and his daughter, Jenny, who had scars on her face and neck and never talked. They said his wife had died in a car accident and wondered why a city guy had come to such a small town and whether the child was mentally handicapped.

Sasha glanced down at the little girl clinging to her father's leg. If the child was four, as she'd heard, she was small for her age. Thin, too. Her bright blue eyes—as blue as her father's—seemed to take up most of her face. They were alert eyes, though. Expressive. The child wasn't mentally handicapped. Sasha would bet on that.

She'd known they would meet sooner or later; had expected that one day Ross Hammond would bring his daughter to her story hour. Now he was here.

Slowly she let her eyes travel back up from daughter to father.

Not overly tall, he had a lean, trim body. His black leather boots, charcoal-gray slacks and natural-colored wool cable-knit sweater could have easily graced a fashion ad, especially one for *GQ*. He appeared to be in his early thirties and was—as the townspeople had said— quite good-looking, his features well-defined, his hair a dark tawny blond, cut quite short in a businessmen's style. She suspected it would curl like his daughter's if allowed to grow any longer.

"Is that the girl that can't talk?" Mandy whispered loudly.

Sasha's attention returned to the children seated in front of her. For a second she'd forgotten them. She'd even forgotten her manners. "Hello," she said, looking back at Jenny and smiling warmly. "Welcome to our story hour. The children were just talking about some of the things they want. Won't you come join us?"

Jenny turned away and buried her face against her father's pant leg.

"Whatsa matter, mister, can't she talk?" Mandy asked bluntly, looking at Ross for an answer.

"Oh, dear. I'm sorry." The woman next to Ross groaned in embarrassment. "My daughter doesn't know the word 'tact'."

He gave Mandy's mother a quick, reassuring smile, then directed his answer to all the children on the rug. "No, Jenny can't talk right now. She was in an accident, and her throat was hurt. But the doctors say she will talk again . . . someday."

"Someday," he'd discovered, was the medical profession's favorite word. The doctors had all been so vague, avoiding definite times or even positive assurances. He'd thought they meant weeks, but it had now been months, and Jenny hadn't uttered a sound—not one. His daughter had learned to communicate by gesturing for things she wanted, and he was beginning to wonder if she would ever speak again.

"What's her name?" asked another girl. Mandy's boldness was encouraging the others.

"Jenny. Actually, it's Jennifer—Jennifer Marie—but we've always called her Jenny." Ross felt ill at ease. Other than at the hospital, this was the first time he'd ever been around many children. Before the accident Donna had always taken Jenny places. She'd had to; he'd never been around.

"Jenny, wouldn't you like to join us?" Sasha asked again.

Ross felt Jenny press harder against his leg.

"Maybe your daddy would like to pull up a chair and sit with us. Then you could sit right in front of him." Sasha looked at Ross for his reaction to the suggestion.

He nodded. It was clear that Jenny wasn't going to join the children on her own. Moving slowly—any other way was impossible with a four-year-old attached to his pant leg—he pulled a chair over next to Mandy and sat down, urging Jenny to sit on the rug beside him.

"What kinda accident was she in?" Mandy asked, leaning toward Jenny and studying the scars on her face.

Jenny inched away, putting herself on the other side of her father's legs. Squeezing her doll close, she buried her face in Anna's brown wool hair.

Ross rested a reassuring hand on Jenny's head. The children's expressions indicated they all wanted to know what had happened. He wasn't really surprised. The adults who saw Jenny were just as curious, but not as forthright in their questions. Carefully he tried to explain. "Jenny was in a car accident. A bad one. A lot of her bones were broken, and she was cut up very badly."

Sasha's heart went out to the child. What that little girl must have gone through. No wonder she looked so frail.

"Will her face get better?" the boy called Toby asked shyly.

"Someday," Ross answered, then grimaced. That word again. He hated it, especially when he thought of the plastic surgery ahead for Jenny. His daughter had been so pretty once.

Sasha was sure it had to be difficult for him to talk about his daughter's accident and tried to change the subject. "Children, maybe Jenny can't talk, but can you say hello to her?"

A chorus of hellos answered her request, the pre-schoolers ready to please.

"Did she ever talk?" persisted Mandy, her curiosity not yet sated.

"Oh, yes. A lot." Ross remembered one evening after dinner when he was working on a brief he'd brought home. Jenny's incessant chatter had driven him crazy, and he'd angrily ordered her to be quiet. Now he'd give anything to hear that high-pitched, childish voice again.

"Did the car hit another car like this?" One of the older boys slapped his hands together to demonstrate a collision.

"No, it went off the road and hit a tree."

"Was you in it?" another child questioned.

"No." He hadn't expected these children to ask so many questions. The ones in the hospital ward hadn't—but then they'd had problems of their own. Perhaps he'd made a mistake in bringing Jenny here. He wasn't sure how much she remembered about the accident, or if talking about it would bring back memories of her mother. He rubbed his hand over her curly brown locks and shifted his weight in the chair. Perhaps it would be best if they left.

Sasha knew he was uneasy. "Children—" she urged their attention back to her "—let's let Jenny and her father get used to us before you ask any more questions. Now, what were we talking about before they came in?"

"Kittens," said Mandy.

"I want a 'am'," a little dark-haired tot sitting cross-legged on the rug insisted. "Awjer da Am."

"Roger the Lamb?" Sasha asked.

The child nodded energetically.

"Does anyone else want to see Roger the Lamb?"

Immediately a chorus of yeses went up.

"Good, because Roger the Lamb wants to see you." The book on her lap was closed, and Sasha turned to one of the cardboard boxes by her side and pulled out a lamb marionette made of wood, stuffed cloth and actual lamb's wool. "Did I ever tell you about the time Roger got lost and Mia and Mike had to find him? One day. . ."

As Sasha told the story, the children forgot about Jenny, and Ross relaxed. The lamb marionette was joined by two dolls, both very similar to Jenny's Anna—one a boy doll, the other a girl. The girl doll, Mia, had short, curly blond hair and green eyes. The boy had straight brown hair and brown eyes. Sasha manipulated the marionette and dolls, using them to help tell her story, and Jenny leaned forward to listen.

AT NOON, SASHA put away her dolls and the marionette and wished each of the children a good week. Ready for lunch, they went quickly to their mothers and started out of the room. Ross stood but didn't leave. He was glad he'd come and glad he'd stayed. For the first time in weeks, Jenny had focused on someone other than him. He'd even seen her smile when Sasha made the lamb dance. It was a start.

With the dolls in their boxes Sasha stood and brushed the folds of her long skirt into place. From beneath the hem only the toes of her black boots could be seen. Ross Hammond and his daughter were still in the room, and it seemed appropriate to greet Putnam's new residents formally. "I'm glad you brought your daughter," she said, moving toward Ross. She held out her right hand. "I imagine you already know it, but I'm Sasha Peters. Some call me the Doll Lady."

"And I'm Ross Hammond." He reached out his hand. "Some call me a lawyer."

"So I've heard." A visible blue-white spark arced between their fingertips, sending a tingle up her arm. Then he wrapped his fingers around hers.

"You're quite electrifying," he said, squeezing gently. And he meant it. It was more than static electricity. Simply being in the room with her was galvanizing.

"I've been getting zapped all morning." Sasha pulled her fingers free and rubbed her hand along the side of her skirt. Strange. She knew the sparking that had occurred between their fingers was merely a matter of too many charged ions in the air, but she wasn't sure how to explain the surge of energy she'd felt when his fingers tightened around hers.

Ross felt a small tug on his pant leg and looked down to find Jenny making a series of gestures. "I think she's trying to say she enjoyed your story."

Sasha crouched so that she was at eye level with the little girl. "Roger the Lamb had quite an adventure, didn't he? He and Mia and Mike have lots of adventures together. And so do the other dolls I've made." Reaching out, she touched the doll Jenny held. "Did you know I made this doll?"

Wide-eyed, Jenny shook her head, hugging Anna closer.

"Oh, don't worry, I wouldn't take her away from you. I can see you love her very much. What's her name?"

"Anna," Ross supplied. "She's named after my sister. Ann bought the doll for Jenny."

Sasha gave him an appreciative smile, then touched the doll's cloth face. "I bet your aunt bought Anna because she looks like you, Jenny. You both have brown hair and blue eyes. But you know what? Your eyes are prettier."

Unexpectedly Jenny reached out and touched Sasha's face. Tiny fingers moved over Sasha's high cheekbones to just below her eyes, then on to her pale yellow curls. Next Jenny waved toward one of the boxes on the floor, then again pointed at Sasha's eyes and hair.

Sasha understood. "Yes, Mia looks like me. Mia means 'mine' or 'my.' We each have a doll that looks like us."

Still holding on to her doll, Jenny wrapped her free arm around Sasha's neck and pressed herself close. Touched by the show of affection and trust, Sasha hugged the child, then stood, holding Jenny in her arms. "She's precious, Mr. Hammond. Absolutely precious."

The picture of his daughter lovingly hugging Sasha lodged a lump in his throat. He had to swallow twice before he could speak. "I've never seen her take to a stranger so readily."

"We're not strangers, are we?" Sasha murmured into Jenny's curls. "We're related. Our dolls are sisters."

Jenny cuddled against Sasha, and Ross watched as his daughter's small hand slid down from Sasha's neck to the front of her dress. Tiny fingers poked curiously at a large, soft breast, and he didn't know what to say or do.

As casually as Sasha could manage, she shifted the child over to her hip, hoping the change in position would resolve the problem. But Jenny merely poked curiously at Sasha's other breast.

This time Sasha turned her back to Ross and took a few steps toward her boxes of dolls. "You're a sweetie," she crooned, slipping her hand over Jenny's to ease the child's fingers back up to her neck.

The older woman who had been behind the desk when Ross came into the library knocked lightly on the door-jamb and cleared her throat. "Will you be much longer, Sasha? I was going to lock up for lunch."

"All through, Emma," Sasha said and turned back to Ross. She grinned as she neared him. "Only in a small town like Putnam does the library close for lunch."

Emma moved back into the other room, and Sasha shifted her hands to Jenny's waist to give the child to Ross. He reached forward to take her, his hands gently spanning his daughter's body. He was about to lift Jenny away when she changed her mind about going and again wrapped her legs around Sasha's waist and her arm around her neck. Suddenly Ross's hands were trapped, his fingers pressed into soft, womanly curves. He could feel the heat of Sasha's body radiating through the coarse wool of her dress, heard her quick intake of breath and was aware that her nipples were hardening against his knuckles. Jenny squeezed tightly, and Ross groaned.

Sasha could have echoed the sound. His touch was triggering an erotic curling in the pit of her stomach, stimulating primitive responses. As he pulled his hands away, the sensation of his fingers rubbing over her nipples sent an exhilarating jolt to all her nerve endings. Even when the contact was broken and he'd stepped back, the effect lingered.

Having a man's hands on her breasts wasn't a new experience for Sasha. Men usually looked for excuses to fondle her. And normally, being pawed disgusted her. But she could tell Ross hadn't intended to touch her, and she found herself wanting to tell him it was all right. The poor man. He looked completely flustered.

"I'm sorry, I didn't mean to . . . That is, she's usually not like this. . . ." His face turned red. "Usually I can't get away from her. Usually she throws herself into my arms."

His discomposure was refreshing. Basically ignoring what had happened, Sasha murmured into Jenny's hair. "Sweetheart, you've got to go to your daddy now. I've got to get my things so the librarian can lock up."

Jenny gave no indication of loosening her grip.

"Come on, Jenny." He certainly wasn't going to try to take her from Sasha again. He wouldn't say he'd minded the feel of those large breasts against the backs of his hands, but he definitely wasn't in the habit of grabbing a woman. To his dismay, his body had responded automatically, and he didn't dare look down for fear of bringing attention to how much he *had* enjoyed the experience.

"Your daddy will bring you back next week." Sasha glanced at Ross, hoping she hadn't misspoken. His nod allowed her to go on. "Next week you can sit by my side and we can tell a story about how Anna and Mia met. Would you like that?"

Jenny nodded, hugging Sasha more tightly.

"Honey, if we go now, Daddy will buy you an ice cream."

That suggestion caught the child's attention, and she leaned back.

Sasha smiled. "That does sound good, doesn't it? My favorite is rocky road. I love all those soft marshmallows. Do you like rocky road?"

Jenny nodded vigorously.

"I'll buy you rocky road," Ross promised.

That was all it took. Jenny twisted toward him, her blue eyes bright with anticipation.

"Thank you, Miss Peters," Ross said when Jenny was finally back in his arms.

"Oh, call me Sasha. Everyone does."

"Sasha." He repeated the name, liking the sound. "Do you hold these story hours anywhere else? Any other day?" He'd gladly take the time and drive a few miles to see Jenny as animated as she was now. To be honest, he'd make the drive for himself. The Doll Lady fascinated him.

"No. Only Wednesdays. The other days I'm busy working on my house and dolls."

"Well, then..." He hesitated, not really wanting to go.

From the corner of his eye he saw the librarian return to the doorway. He was glad the woman hadn't come back sooner. He could imagine how it would have looked—his hands on Sasha's breasts. Considering how fast gossip traveled in this town, that sight would have had tongues wagging.

"Well, see you around," he said, but still didn't move. He couldn't pull his eyes away from Sasha's.

"See you around," she repeated softly.

The librarian cleared her throat, and Ross knew he couldn't put off his departure any longer. Reluctantly he turned away, nodding at the librarian as he passed.

Sasha waited until Ross and Jenny left before she picked up her cardboard boxes. She was already thinking about next Wednesday. She'd bring Clancy the Clown. He always made the children laugh. Jenny would enjoy him. Maybe even Ross would smile. He looked so sad.

The boxes pressed against her breasts, and Sasha closed her eyes, remembering the momentary touch of

Ross's hands. A quivery, fluttery sensation stirred deep inside her body, and she suddenly felt very warm. Surprised by her reaction, Sasha blinked open her eyes and found Emma watching her, smiling.

2

SASHA PUSHED HER grocery cart down the paper-products aisle, her mind on the telephone call she'd received that morning, not on her shopping. Benson Toys wanted her doll. One of the largest toy manufacturers in America wanted the rights to the My Friends dolls. It was unbelievable. A product of her imagination would one day be in stores across the nation, maybe throughout the world. Like Xavier Roberts's Cabbage Patch dolls, her old-fashioned cloth dolls might one day be a household word.

That would show her father.

Darn it all, Sasha realized, she didn't have to show her father anything. It was Orrie Peters's problem that he'd never accepted who she was, not hers.

Not that being Orrie Peters's daughter hadn't been a problem. There had been many times when she was growing up that she'd wished she was like her sister, Tanya. If she'd been studious, sensible and willing to do as her father asked, life in the Peters household would have been easier. As it was, she'd spent a lot of hours isolated in her room to "think things over." Thank goodness she'd had an active imagination. The My Friends dolls had been created in that bedroom. She'd egotistically called the first one Sasha's Doll until she looked through a doll collectors' magazine and discovered there already was a Sasha Doll. So she changed the name to

My Friends. And in reality that was what the dolls were becoming.

After her big blowup with her father it was the My Friends dolls that subsidized her day-to-day existence. Now it looked as though they were going to provide a very lucrative livelihood. No more scrimping to make ends meet. She'd have money to fix up her house. Lots of money. That sounded good to Sasha. With a carefree burst of energy she zipped her cart around the corner.

Metal banged into metal.

"Ohh!" She grunted, the jolt of hitting another cart taking her breath away.

"Dammit, why don't you watch where you're going!" Ross Hammond snapped, not even looking to see who'd run into his cart. His concern was for his daughter. "Are you all right, honey? Did you hit your chin on the bar? Your throat?" Quickly he checked Jenny's face and neck. If she was hurt he'd—

Frantically Jenny pulled away from his touch, motioning toward the floor. At first he didn't understand, then he looked down and saw Anna in a heap at his feet.

Jenny's concern for her doll relieved him, and Ross bent to retrieve Anna. From his stooped position he could see the hem of a blue gingham dress above the toes of a pair of black high-heeled boots. The familiar pattern of the gingham didn't register. All he knew was that this was the defendant, and his temper flared. "Lady, what do you think this is, the Indy 500? Why weren't you looking where you were going?"

"Why were you on my side of the aisle?" Sasha returned. She wasn't about to take the blame for something that wasn't entirely her fault. "Are you all right, Jenny?"

At the sound of Sasha's voice Jenny turned in the seat of the cart, a broad smile breaking across her face.

Ross stood, doll in hand. He didn't know what to say. A part of him was still angry, but realizing he'd run into Sasha—and seeing how happy Jenny was to see her— balanced that anger.

Sasha wiggled her nose at Jenny, and the child held out her arms, gesturing for Sasha to pick her up.

"Well, maybe I was on the wrong side...but you were going too fast," Ross said, but not very emphatically.

If he was willing to admit he'd been wrong, so was she. "You're right. I was going too fast, and I'm sorry. My mind was on something else. You're sure you're okay, honey?" She pushed her cart aside and stepped closer to Jenny.

The child wiggled to a kneeling position, her arms outstretched.

"May I?" Sasha asked Ross.

Jenny didn't give him a chance to answer. Before either Sasha or Ross could react, Jenny jumped from the grocery cart.

"Well, hi." Sasha grunted as the child's light body hit against her breasts. Quickly she wrapped her arms around the little girl.

Ross could only stare. Holding Jenny, Sasha reminded him of Mother Goose—a young Mother Goose.

Her floor-length dress and matching cloth bonnet were an exact duplicate of the dress and bonnet on the doll in his hand. Only Sasha filled out the dress a lot more provocatively than the doll did. Jenny snuggled against the soft pillow of Sasha's breasts and Ross remembered how nice they'd felt, pressed against his hands. Quickly he brought his eyes back up to her face.

She'd noticed the direction his gaze had traveled—and its quick retreat. Their eyes met, and she smiled.

"Do you always wear a long dress when you go out?" he asked, a bit flustered.

"At home or out. I started wearing them ten years ago as a promotional gimmick for my dolls. Now people expect to see me in one."

Different but understandable. Standard attire for him in Sacramento had been a Brooks Brothers suit. People had expected to see him dressed that way, and right now he wished he had one on. When he'd left his house for the store, he hadn't thought to change out of his grimy sweatshirt and jeans. This was to have been a quick trip for sandwich goodies, a few minutes' break from sawing wood and pounding nails. So who did he run into? It didn't seem fair.

Ever since leaving the library Wednesday, he'd been thinking about Sasha Peters. No matter what he did, he couldn't seem to get the woman out of his mind. Her face had even haunted his dreams. It was crazy.

He tried to brush some of the sawdust and dirt off his right sleeve. "Sorry, I've been working on my house . . . making bookshelves."

"I imagine a lawyer has a lot of books." Actually Sasha liked the way he looked, less like a fashion-magazine advertisement, more approachable. The scent of sawdust, sweat and maleness surrounded him, and she found it pleasant, stimulating.

Jenny remembered her doll and turned in Sasha's arms to reach back to her father.

He handed her the doll, and Jenny again snuggled close to Sasha, Anna's dress blending right in with Sasha's. "You know, when the waitress over at the café told me you'd made that doll, I didn't believe her," Ross admitted. "What a coincidence."

"Oh, not that big a coincidence, really. My dolls are sold in boutiques all over northern California. A lot of children who come through Putnam have them." Soon children all across the United States might have dolls like Jenny's Anna and her Mia. Sasha was tempted to tell Ross her good news, then decided to wait. She needed to think about the offer.

"Well, I can't begin to tell you how much my daughter loves that doll." He wondered if the warm feelings he had for Sasha were because of his gratitude.

"I'm glad."

"She won't let it out of her sight."

"You'll have to bring Jenny out to my place sometime. I think she'd like meeting the other dolls and animals I've made." Sasha spoke softly to Jenny. "Mia and Mike would love to have a tea party for Anna. Would she like that?"

Jenny looked at her doll, nodded as if the doll had spoken to her, then turned back to Sasha and nodded.

"How about this afternoon?" Ross heard himself asking.

SASHA MADE A PITCHER of lemonade, then brought a half dozen of her favorite dolls outside to a foot-high table. Each doll was placed in a small specially made chair, and a miniature cup and saucer set in front of each of them. Tea parties were always fun. The children loved them. She hadn't held one for a long time. Every since she'd started the story hour at the library three years before, she'd made a habit each month of inviting a few of the children to afternoon tea. It had given her a chance to get to know each child better.

In the house she'd shared with her sister, Tanya, Sasha had held the tea parties on their enclosed porch year-round, but after her sister announced her engagement, there'd been no time for such things. Sasha had been too busy helping with the wedding arrangements and looking for a place for herself.

She'd always been attracted to the old one-story house nestled in the glen just outside of town, and since moving in she'd been busy making the place livable. Now she had one room where she could safely entertain young children, and with the weather growing warmer, as it was today, she could hold the tea parties outside.

The townspeople, she knew, considered it odd that a grown woman would hold tea parties for children. Actually she was sure most of the residents around Putnam considered her a kook, but she didn't care. She loved what she was doing. Nothing pleased her more than bringing a smile to a child's face.

Sasha was getting a plate of oatmeal cookies when Ross steered his flashy silver-and-black BMW down the steep gravel drive that led to her yard. Nero, the three-legged black Labrador retriever she'd found lying by the side of the road two years before, the victim of a hit-and-run, ran out barking, his tail wagging. Not far behind came Polo, the salt-and-pepper poodle mix that had been left behind by summer campers. For every deep bark that Nero gave, Polo added a high-pitched yip. The pair never failed to warn her when someone arrived.

"Welcome to Never-Neverland," she greeted as Ross got out of the car. "Here you must put aside your adult ideas and become a child again."

He paused to look around, the two dogs sniffing at his pant legs. The old frame house looked as though it might fall apart any second. Siding was missing, most of the windows were boarded up and the front porch, with a Stay Off sign hanging from a broken railing, sloped precariously. She'd said she was working on her house, yet he hadn't expected to find it in such bad shape. Put aside his adult ideas? He couldn't. Children might enjoy playing in run-down houses; as an adult he could see the dangers.

Sasha followed Ross's gaze as his blue eyes flitted over the house. She wondered how he saw her home. Sure, the house needed fixing up, but she could do most of the work herself. It was only a matter of time and money. She had the time, and if the deal with the toy company panned out, she'd have the money.

Otherwise, the place was exactly what she wanted. Set below and away from the main road, surrounded by trees and craggy slopes of granite, her patch of open land offered the privacy she'd learned to treasure. Crocuses and daffodils were now coming up, and in just a few more weeks the rosebushes growing under the kitchen window would start to bloom. Soon she'd plant a garden. She loved beautiful flowers and fresh vegetables. And animals. As a child she'd begged for a dog or a cat. Her father had said no, they weren't practical. Now she could have her animals, practical or not.

"Have you been working on this place long?" Ross asked hesitantly, not quite sure how to express his reaction to the ramshackle house.

"A little over four months. Never-Neverland's a bit run-down, but I think it has a lot of potential."

"'A bit run-down'?" His eyebrows rose.

His thoughts were all too evident, and Sasha's chin lifted slightly. His reaction was exactly what she should have expected. Exactly what her father's would be if he ever saw the place. *Dump it*, he'd say. *Get a decent house . . . a decent job.* Some men simply had no imagination, couldn't see that in a few months, with the windows and siding replaced, the porch repaired and the flower bed weeded and in bloom, the house would look like something straight out of a storybook. "It's got potential," she repeated, and walked past him to greet Jenny.

The child was buckled into her seat, her doll on her lap. As Sasha neared, Jenny smiled.

"I couldn't get her to take a nap this afternoon," said Ross, coming around to open the door. "She's been so excited since we ran into you in the store."

Sasha wondered if he was emphasizing the point that she'd literally run into him.

He hesitated before releasing Jenny's seat belt. "Will we be going inside your house?"

"It's warmed up enough that I have the tea party set up outside, but I thought we might go into the living room later. I have the marionettes stored there."

She could read the concern on his face. "Really, Mr. Hammond, my house is quite safe. The structure's sound—as long as you stay off the porch." She was a little irked that he didn't trust her. "I'd never bring a child into a place that wasn't safe." That's why she hadn't invited any of the story-hour children over. Until just this week she hadn't had a room finished where she could entertain without worrying about them picking up nails or other building materials.

Ross wasn't entirely convinced that he wasn't subjecting his daughter to a dangerous situation, yet he didn't know what else to do. If he didn't stay, Jenny would be heartbroken. He released the seat belt and lifted her into his arms.

With a new body on the scene the two dogs immediately renewed their investigation, Nero sniffing at Jenny's patent-leather shoes and Polo yipping and jumping around on his hind legs. Her blue eyes wide, Jenny looked down at the dogs. Wrapping one arm around her father's neck, she pulled her knees up to her chest.

But in the process of trying to escape the dogs, her grip on Anna loosened. The doll began to slip. Jenny twisted in Ross's arms, grabbing for the doll. Nero's nose touched her small hand, and Jenny opened her mouth and jerked back her arm.

The cloth doll hit the dirt, and Polo immediately stopped jumping about to sniff the fallen object. Nero, too, left Ross's side to check out Polo's find.

Terror contorted Jenny's face, her mouth still open, her eyes relaying her fear that the dogs were going to destroy her precious Anna.

"I think I heard a sound! I think she said something," Ross cried, hugging his daughter close and burying his face in her soft curls. He hoped he had. It had been so long.

Sasha hadn't heard a word, but she could understand what Jenny was going through. She'd been ten years old the day her father grabbed the first doll she'd actually made from her sketched designs. "A waste of time," he'd shouted. "You'll never succeed in this world, playing with dolls. Now, get to work on your math."

Quickly Sasha bent down and retrieved Anna. With a shake and a pat she removed the dust from the doll's dress and cloth body, then handed her back to Jenny. "Nero and Polo wouldn't hurt Anna. They just wanted to make sure she was all right and say hello. They won't hurt you, either, Jenny."

Ross was staring at his daughter. "Jenny, can you talk?"

Jenny made no sound but looked down at the two dogs. The fear left her eyes. She didn't relinquish her hold on her father, though, and she hugged Anna close.

"Jenny, talk to Daddy," he persisted desperately.

She looked back at his face, then gently pressed a finger against his lips. In a second her attention returned to the dogs. Curiously she watched Nero limp away on his three legs, off on a new quest. Polo trotted faithfully behind. A gray-and-white tiger cat peeked out from under a scraggly juniper, and Nero picked up his pace, moving in the direction of the cat. Sasha knew the chase would soon be on.

"I'm sure I heard a sound," Ross insisted, his initial buoyancy waning.

"Maybe you did." Sasha only knew she hadn't. "Would you like to join Mia and Mike for tea?" she asked Jenny. She could see no use in pressing the matter. When Jenny was ready to talk, she would talk.

The little girl nodded.

Sasha took them to where she'd set up the dolls. She'd left two empty chairs between Mia and Mike. Anna was placed in one. Jenny held back from taking the other chair until Ross assured her he'd sit on the flagstones right behind her. Then Jenny joined the dolls at the table.

For a while Sasha entertained Jenny, pouring her a glass of lemonade and passing her the plate of cookies. She introduced each of the dolls and told a bit about its personal life and the adventures it had had. Seated behind his daughter, Ross watched and listened, fascinated.

Sasha was still wearing the blue gingham dress she'd had on at the store, and she still reminded him of Mother Goose. Crazy, he thought. *If she believes these stories she's telling, she's got to be crazy.*

But also lovely.

Pale blond curls framed her delicate features. The light color was duplicated in her eyebrows, and her peaches-and-cream complexion matched her fairness. In contrast, her eyes were a startling green flecked with gold. As she pretended to pour more tea for the dolls, he studied her hands. She had long, slender fingers, small knuckles and . . .

He frowned. Her hands definitely weren't her prettiest feature. Her nails were short and ragged, and around the quicks he saw traces of brown stain. She also had an ugly bruise on her left thumb. Having hit his thumb with his hammer just that morning, he had an inkling of how she'd gotten her bruise. He wondered if she played carpenter in a long dress.

It had been a long time since he'd met a woman who wore a dress—a dress of any length—around the house. Donna had worn them when entertaining for him but always said she preferred the comfort and freedom of movement that pants provided. Personally, he preferred a woman in shorts. They showed off her legs best. He wondered what Sasha's legs looked like.

She leaned over to pour more lemonade into Jenny's glass, and Ross's eyes were drawn to the cleavage visible above the scoop of her neckline. He might be a leg man, but he would have to be blind not to appreciate Sasha's other attributes. The memory of touching her breasts triggered a tightening in his groin. Oh, great, he silently groaned, and shifted slightly. He wondered how many men got erections at children's tea parties. But then, not too many would have an alluring Mother Goose bending over right in front of them.

Sasha straightened and caught him staring at her breasts. In her sweetest, most innocent tone she asked, "Would you like something?"

Ross swallowed hard. Yes, he wanted something—her—and that surprised him.

"Tea, coffee, or . . . ?"

Or me? he waited for her to say.

"—Water?" she finished after a poignant pause.

He cleared his throat, his face feeling very hot. "Coffee would be fine, if you have some." The words came out more gravelly than he'd expected.

He was blushing again, and she loved it. "It'll have to be instant."

"Instant's fine," he said, then quickly turned his attention to Jenny. It was safer.

Sasha watched him fuss over his daughter for a moment, then she smiled. "I'll go put on the water. Keep an eye on the food. If the dogs realize there are cookies around, they'll be here in a minute."

Ross waited until she'd gone into the house, then he closed his eyes and took a deep, calming breath. What was wrong with him? A woman entertained his daughter, and he started thinking of making love. It was crazy. Sasha Peters was crazy. He was crazy.

Maybe the waitress had been right. Perhaps he did need some adult companionship. As soon as he had the work on his office finished and Jenny felt more secure, he'd find a baby-sitter for Jenny and a woman for himself.

IN THE KITCHEN Sasha put on the teakettle and lit the gas burner. The afternoon was turning out to be fun. She was thoroughly enjoying entertaining Jenny. The child was so receptive, her eyes saying what her voice could not.

It was always a pleasure for Sasha to tell her stories to an attentive audience.

And Ross. His eyes were also very expressive. She could tell when his thoughts turned to sex. She was also sure he thought she was off her rocker, and she knew he didn't approve of her house.

Sasha looked around the room she was in. The kitchen needed new linoleum, new wallpaper and a new sink and countertop, but she'd already refinished the cupboards and replaced the two windows. Remodeling an old house took time, but she was getting there.

Through the window next to her butcher-block table, she could see out onto the patio. Ross was watching Jenny offer a cookie to her Anna. As Sasha waited for the water to boil, she studied him.

He'd changed from the jeans and sweatshirt he'd been wearing that morning to dark gray slacks, a lighter gray sports jacket and a blue-striped oxford-cloth shirt that was open at the neck. At least he hadn't worn a tie, but he still looked too formal to be sitting on flagstones. Maybe she should bring him one of the kitchen chairs. It would be nice if she had a few lawn chairs. She'd have to buy some as soon as she had some money.

Money.

She'd always argued with her father that it wasn't everything, but one thing she'd learned in her twenty-eight years was that money did make life easier. It was certainly necessary for paying the bills. If she signed the contract with Benson Toys, she'd have money. Lots of it. But should she sign? She'd been giving the matter a lot of thought since morning. She didn't want to make a mistake.

Her gaze still on Ross, she nodded to herself. He was a lawyer. Maybe he could help her. At least she could ask his advice. It would be worth a lawyer's fee not to get trapped by a lot of legal jargon.

The dogs came around the corner of the house, tongues hanging out, and Sasha grinned. That tomcat must have given them quite a run. When Nero saw Jenny and Ross, his tail began to wag. Eagerly the Lab headed toward the low table, Polo following. Ross moved protectively closer to his daughter, and Sasha hoped he wouldn't have any trouble keeping the dogs away from the cookies. They could be pests.

She watched, ready to go back outside if necessary, but Ross acted as a shield between the dogs and his daughter. Soon he had both dogs sitting, obediently waiting for Jenny to feed them a bite of cookie. Smiling, Sasha turned back to the stove. Ross Hammond was a good father—protective and concerned, but willing to allow his daughter the freedom to experience life. The love he felt for Jenny was obvious. Poor guy—to lose his wife and almost lose his daughter. She could understand why he never smiled.

She'd gotten a smile from Jenny—several, in fact. Now she wanted to get one from Ross. The kettle whistled, and Sasha turned off the flame.

When she returned to the patio carrying Ross's coffee, Nero and Polo were both seated next to Jenny, patiently waiting for bites of cookie. Ross was still beside his daughter, watching, but he wasn't intervening.

"I'm afraid that's the last of the cookies," he confessed, looking up when Sasha stopped by his side. "I thought Jenny would get over her fear of the dogs if she saw they weren't going to hurt her. I was just going to have her feed them a couple of the cookies, but one bite seemed to lead to another."

Sasha chuckled. She could certainly understand that. "Same thing always happens to me. Nero's the big one. He's the leader of the two. Polo's the follower. They love it when I have a tea party. They know they'll get most of the cookies." She handed Ross an old-fashioned flower-patterned porcelain cup and saucer. "I forgot to ask if you take cream and sugar."

"Black." Carefully he took the delicate cup and saucer she offered. His hand shook a little.

While she'd been gone, he'd tried to convince himself it wasn't Sasha personally he wanted—just a woman. Yet, since moving to Putnam, he'd met several attractive women, many eager to let him know they were available; but none had interested him. Sasha did, however, and that was an unnerving realization.

Polo got the last of the cookies. Nero nuzzled Jenny's hand, and the child looked at Sasha for a response.

"No, that's enough for those two pigs. They'd eat every cookie I baked if I'd let them. Would you like to go inside and meet the marionettes?"

Jenny nodded, affectionately petting Nero's soft muzzle. Ross tensed.

Sasha sensed his concern. "Don't worry. It's perfectly safe in there." Without giving him a chance to argue, she began picking up her dolls. "Bring Anna and Mia with you, Jenny. I'll get the others. We can leave the cups and saucers until later."

Ross couldn't think of an excuse to stop the proceedings. He hoped Sasha was right—that it was safe inside. Carrying his cup and saucer, he followed them into the house.

Once through the door, he was surprised to find the living room a decorator's dream. Knotty pine walls were polished to a shine, the hardwood floor had been sanded smooth, then varnished and covered with beautiful handwoven rag rugs. From rough-hewn ceiling rafters hung two brass lanterns, while a variety of kerosene lamps, in different styles and colors, sat on the wide marble mantel above the stone fireplace.

The furnishings were few—a rocking chair, a chintz-covered sofa and a lacquered pine-burl coffee table. *Mother Earth* magazines, along with books on gardening and knitting, lay in a basket beside the hearth. Next to the rocking chair was a tapestry bag, from which peeked two long needles and a skein of blue yarn. In one corner of the room was a sewing machine; in another, a large black steamer trunk decorated with colorful tole flowers. Sasha headed directly for the trunk, with Jenny close behind.

First the dolls—except for Anna, who stayed in Jenny's arms—were set around the base of the trunk. Then Sasha opened the lid and reached inside.

One by one she pulled marionettes of varying sizes and shapes out of the trunk. Ross sat down on the sofa to drink his coffee and watch. Occasionally Jenny looked over to make sure he was still there, but she was content to stay with Sasha. It was a step in the right direction, he knew, yet her independence bothered him. He was changing his life for her, and already she was deserting him.

Immediately he corrected his thinking. He wasn't changing his life for Jenny; he was changing it for himself. A man who didn't even know what he was missing in life had no life. Work. That's all he'd known until six months ago. Long hours, close attention to detail, and dogged determination—he'd believed those objectives would bring him success, and that success would buy happiness. How wrong he'd been.

Ross lifted his cup to his lips, only to discover he'd finished the last drop. Sasha was involved in telling a story while Jenny listened, fascinated. He didn't want to disturb them, so he quietly headed for the kitchen. He could fix his own coffee.

"JENNY FELL ASLEEP on the dolls," Sasha announced softly, stepping into the kitchen. Her throat was dry after so much constant talking, and she moved toward the stove to heat some water for a cup of tea. At least during her weekly story hour she got a break when the children interrupted to ask questions or add their own comments. Jenny was a silent audience.

Ross turned from the newly refinished cabinets he'd been inspecting in time to see Sasha jerk her hand back from the kettle. "Sorry, I should have warned you. The water should still be hot. I hope you don't mind, but I fixed myself some more coffee." He set his cup down on the stained and worn counter, having left the saucer in the sink earlier. Mugs were his style. "I suppose I should get her home."

"I covered her with an afghan. Why don't you let her sleep for a while before you disturb her." Sasha blew on her fingertips, then reached for the jar that held her favorite blend of tea. She wanted to talk to Ross.

"Maybe I will let her sleep for a while," he decided. It had been a pleasant afternoon—a break from the work he'd been doing remodeling the front room, and a good experience for his daughter. Besides, when a man had such a lovely hostess, why leave?

"More coffee?" she asked.

"Sounds good." Picking up his cup again, he stepped over to the stove, where he'd left the jar of instant and the spoon he'd used earlier. Side by side they worked, Sasha preparing her tea, Ross fixing his coffee.

She smelled good to him—of fresh air and sunshine, a touch of bath powder and an aroma that was delightfully feminine. Absently stirring his coffee, he looked at her.

There was something almost chimerical about Sasha Peters. Everything about her delighted him—her soft, singsong voice, the way she dressed and her beautiful face. Maybe his thoughts didn't make sense, but he'd definitely love to hold her in his arms . . . kiss her lovely lips.

Sasha glanced up to find him staring at her face, his eyes devouring her. She'd seen the hungry, adoring look in other men's eyes, and she knew what it meant. *Please, don't*, she wanted to cry. *Don't complicate matters. All I want is to be your friend.*

Yet even as she entertained the thought, her stomach was turning queasy, her knees weak. What would it be like to be kissed by a man like Ross Hammond? Made love to by him? *Don't think such thoughts*, she ordered herself and quickly poured her tea. Turning her back to him, she headed for the butcher-block table. She needed to sit down.

"Sasha?" He wasn't sure what to say. He wasn't even sure what he was feeling. This wasn't the time to get involved with anyone, yet around this woman his senses were coming alive.

"What do you think of my kitchen?" The tension between them was palpable. She had to keep the conversation on safe ground.

"Not bad." He forced himself not to think about kissing her and glanced around the room. "You've got a lot of work ahead of you, though."

Picking up his cup, he carried it over to the table. There he sat across from her. "You're right. This old house does have potential. One thing I always remembered about Putnam was the old houses."

"Remembered? You lived here before?"

"No. Not lived, but I used to come here."

He told her about the hunting trips he'd taken with his uncle and the fond memories he'd held for so many years. "I was a little afraid I'd be disappointed once I moved here, but I haven't been. Everyone's been great. My neighbors even brought over food the first few days after I moved in. Said it was the custom. You know, I didn't even know my neighbors in Sacramento. What a difference."

"I know what you mean." Sasha grinned and took a sip of her tea. "It's called Putnam hospitality." She liked it.

"Have you always lived here?" He wondered if they'd met before, years before. That would have been a coincidence.

"No, I moved up here three years ago. I was born and raised in Oakland."

"And what brought you to Putnam?"

"My sister." Sasha put down her cup and explained. "Tanya is a teacher here. First grade. Soon after she got the job and moved to Putnam, she began writing to me about the town. It sounded so interesting—living in the Sierra foothills, in the heart of the mother-lode country. When I came up for a visit, it was love at first sight. And when Tanya suggested I move in with her, it didn't take me long to make up my mind."

Her short visit had also made her realize that she and her sister had more in common than she'd ever known. "As soon as I got back to Oakland, I found someone to take over the lease on my apartment, then I packed up my sewing machine, dolls and marionettes and headed for the mountains. I lived with Tanya for almost three years.... Then she kicked me out."

Before Ross could say anything, Sasha explained, smiling. "Tanya got married Christmas Day, and I agree with the old saying, 'Two's company, but three's a crowd.' Actually I'd had my eye on this place for some time and was glad to have an excuse to make an offer. The owner gave me a great deal."

Considering the property's run-down condition, he hoped so. "And now you're on your own?"

"Again. I have been since I turned eighteen."

"No man in your life?" He hoped not, for his sake.

"Nope. This is one lady who doesn't want a man running her life."

Her response surprised him. "Running your life?"

"Oh, you know what I mean. Men like to think of themselves as boss of the house." She'd certainly seen that firsthand. "Or if a man's not bossy, he's a wimp." For a while she'd thought she might like to be in control, give the orders instead of having them given to her, but it didn't take her long to discover she couldn't respect a man who allowed that.

"So which am I?"

"Which are you what?"

"Wimp or bossy?"

She didn't see him as a wimp. "Come on, now, do you really need to ask? I'll bet you at least tried to run your wife's life, didn't you?"

Ross blanched at the suggestion. Perhaps if he *had* tried to run Donna's life, had paid more attention to her—any attention to her—things would have turned out differently.

Sasha saw him pale and immediately wished she'd kept her mouth shut. What an oaf she was. She'd wanted to make him smile; instead, she was bringing him sorrow. "I'm sorry. I wasn't thinking. I'm sure you were a wonderful husband. You're a great father to Jenny."

He laughed bitterly, and his gaze met hers. "Wonderful husband? Great father? Do you realize the reason Donna's dead and Jenny can't talk is because of me?"

3

"BECAUSE OF YOU?" Sasha repeated. His statement didn't make sense. In the library Ross had said he wasn't in the car when the accident occurred.

He took in a deep breath, wishing there was a way to banish the feelings of guilt. He couldn't look Sasha in the eyes, so he cradled his coffee cup in his hands and stared down at it. "You say I'm a great father. Well, I don't know about now, but up until six months ago I was a lousy father. And a lousy husband. Worse than lousy. I wasn't driving that car when it went off the road, but I might as well have been. I drove them away."

The pain of his remorse was evident in his expression. "Want to talk about it?" Sasha asked softly.

The night of Donna's funeral, after Ross had returned to the hospital to take up his vigil by his daughter's bedside, he'd broken down and told his sister what had happened. Ann was the only one who knew the full story. He wasn't ready to confess all to Sasha, but he did want her to understand where he was and why.

Slowly Ross raised his head, and gazed at her. He chose his words carefully. "You are looking at a man who placed success in business over love and family. Up until six months ago my credo was 'Work hard, succeed—and you'll be happy.' And I believed it through and through. It wasn't until I saw Jenny in that hospital bed that I realized I was a thirty-three-year-old failure.

"You know, I don't even remember when she got her first tooth. I wasn't around when she took her first steps; I was in Los Angeles negotiating a contract. It was a big step in my career. *My career*. Sasha, for as long as I can recall, that's all I thought about—advancing my career. An eleven-month-old baby's first steps didn't count."

She knew they did now.

"As for running my wife's life . . ." He shook is head. "A man has to be around to do that. I rarely was. Donna and I were strangers living in the same house. I never should have married her." And he wouldn't have, if he hadn't seen it as a good career move.

"I still remember the night we met. I was attending a dinner party put on by one of the law firm's senior partners. Donna was a family friend of his. We sat next to each other at the table and talked. I decided she was an attractive, intelligent, levelheaded woman who would be a good hostess and a good mother for my children. We were married five months later."

To Sasha it sounded too analytical. "What about love? Didn't you love her?"

Once again he looked down, away from her probing eyes. The minister, when he came to call after the accident, had asked the same question. Ross gave Sasha the same answer. "I don't know if I know how to love."

"You love Jenny," she said decisively. She'd seen it in his eyes and in his actions.

Glancing up, he nodded. "Yes, I do. Now." Maybe there was hope for him.

"And even if you didn't love your wife, you must have been the kind of husband she wanted." Who could account for tastes? She certainly couldn't understand why her mother stayed married to her father.

Ross closed his eyes. The memory of a letter, so short and to the point, made his fingers tighten around his coffee cup. With a sharp crack the porcelain gave under the pressure of his fingers.

The cup had broken.

Immediately he dropped the jagged pieces and scooted his chair back, shocked by what he'd done. Hot coffee spread across the top of the butcher-block table, flowing toward the edge.

"Are you all right?" Sasha cried, jumping up to grab a towel.

"I'm sorry." Numbly Ross stared down at the broken pieces of porcelain. He'd crushed her cup. With his fingers alone he'd shattered it. It was probably an antique.

"You cut yourself," she said, concerned. He seemed dazed.

Looking at his hands, he realized there was blood oozing from a cut on his right thumb.

"Let me see it," Sasha ordered. The towel she held was dropped on the tabletop, and she took Ross's hand in hers. Squeezing his thumb to stop the bleeding, she also checked for bits of porcelain that might have lodged in the cut. "Does it hurt?"

"No." He didn't feel anything but the pressure of her fingers...and her warmth and concern. "I'm sorry. I...I'm afraid I owe you a new cup."

"Don't worry about the cup. Come with me." Still holding on to his thumb, she urged him to get up and led him to the sink. There she turned on the water. "This may sting." As gently as she could, she ran water over the cut to clean it.

Ross stared at the top of Sasha's head. She'd made him think of the past. He'd thought he'd come to terms with what had happened with Donna. Obviously he hadn't. "She left me," he said, as much to himself as to her.

Sasha paused in cleaning the cut to look up at him.

"She left me a letter saying she'd met someone else and wanted a divorce . . . and all I wondered was how it was going to affect my career."

He was looking right through her, and Sasha knew he was still very troubled by what had happened. She didn't interrupt.

"I should have gone after her . . ." There was a catch in his voice. "But I didn't. Two days later the guy ran his car into a tree, and they both died."

His sad blue eyes stirred feelings of compassion in Sasha. She reached up and touched his cheek. "You can't change the past, Ross . . . and you can't keep blaming yourself. Your daughter's life was spared. She's the one who needs your love now. Forget yesterday, hope for tomorrow and make today the best ever." It was her philosophy.

He looked at her, really seeing her for the first time since he'd broken the cup. And he smiled.

It was just a half smile, but Sasha was pleased. The tension in his features was easing.

Suddenly Ross realized his thumb was getting very cold under the stream of water, and he moved it. "'Hope for tomorrow and make today the best ever,' eh? Well, today I've hit my left thumb with a hammer and cut this one with a cup. I do hope tomorrow's better."

"You've also had a crazy lady run into your cart in the grocery store." She turned off the water and handed him a paper towel. "Dry that off and I'll get you a Band-Aid."

She started to move away, but he stopped her with a hand on her arm. "A nice crazy lady. Thank you, Sasha.

And thanks for listening to my confession. I guess I didn't want you thinking I was something I wasn't."

Despite what he'd told her—or maybe because of it— she liked him. Years of living with a father who would never admit he'd made a mistake made honesty a precious trait to her. "I think you're a nice guy, Ross Hammond," she said truthfully. "A nice guy who's trying to be better than he was. I'd like to be your friend."

"And I'd like to be yours."

Gently he squeezed her arm, and Sasha felt warm all over. For a second she stood mesmerized, simply staring at his face. Then, shaken, she turned and moved away.

Ross watched her leave the room, her steps smooth and graceful, her long skirt just clearing the floor. Yes, he wanted to be her friend . . . and maybe more.

Sasha returned in a minute with the Band-Aid. Taking his hand in hers, she looked at the cut again. "It's not very deep. I don't think you need stitches."

"It's fine. I'll survive." He watched her carefully apply the small bandage. Her touch was so gentle, her presence soothing. He wanted to wrap his arms around her and hold her close. Instead, he stood very still and simply enjoyed being near her.

With a final pat on the back of his hand she smiled up at him. "That should take care of that."

"About the cup—"

"Forget the cup," she insisted. "However, you can clean up your mess."

Looking over at the table, he noticed the towel had soaked up most of the spilled coffee, but there was a small pool of dark liquid on the worn linoleum under the table. With a nod he walked back to the table.

He was throwing the broken pieces of porcelain away when Jenny came into the kitchen, her eyes still heavy with sleep, her doll clutched in one hand. "Well, Sleeping Beauty, decide it was time to wake up?" he asked gently. Going over to his daughter, he squatted in front of her and tenderly brushed a few tendrils of brown curly hair back from her face. "Ready to go home?"

Looking at Sasha, Jenny shook her head.

Ross also looked at Sasha. He didn't blame his daughter. He'd also like to spend more time with the Doll Lady, but he didn't want to overstay his welcome. It was getting late in the afternoon.

"I'm glad you had a good time," responded Sasha. She came over and stood next to them. "You'll have to get your daddy to bring you again."

Picking Jenny up, Ross straightened and faced her. "You wouldn't mind?"

"Of course not." Sasha reached over to brush the backs of her fingers over Jenny's scarred cheek. "I love entertaining children with my dolls and puppets." She glanced at the doll in Jenny's arms. "Which reminds me, Mr. Hammond, when will you be taking clients?"

"Hey, we're friends, remember? Call me Ross. I should have my office set up in a couple of weeks. Why?"

"I think I need a lawyer." Sasha grinned, unable to suppress her excitement. "I think I've sold My Friends dolls."

"Your friend's dolls?" He frowned, confused.

"The dolls I make. The ones like Anna. Benson Toys wants to buy the design, mass-produce the dolls and sell them in stores all over the country. . . maybe all over the world."

Now he understood. Her dolls were being sought by a nationally known company. "Congratulations."

"Thanks. The problem is, I'm worried."

"About what?"

"I don't want them—Benson Toys—changing the dolls into something crass and commercial."

"Sasha, remember, the company's out to make money. Any way you look at it, if they buy the design, your doll is going to be commercial."

"I know, but I—" She groped for the right words to express her fears. "I don't want the dolls turned into something cheap, something I wouldn't be proud to claim I originated."

"You want to retain some artistic control." He understood and could see her point. In her position he'd want the same. He was impressed that she wasn't jumping at the idea of making a lot of money. Most creative people, he'd found, signed a contract, then discovered they'd given away too much.

"Yes, artistic control." She liked the sound of that. "Can I have artistic control?"

"You can have anything both parties agree to. We don't need to wait until my office is finished. If you'll give me the contract, I'll look at it tonight and see what they're offering."

"I don't have a contract. At least, not yet. Mr. Bernstein—he's the man who called this morning—said it would be mailed to me."

"All right. Then I'll look it over as soon as you get it."

"Great!" It seemed a godsend that a lawyer had moved into town just when she needed one. "Do I need to pay you a retainer?"

"Between friends, a handshake will do." Shifting Jenny to his side, he held out his hand.

The bandage on his thumb rubbed against her skin, and she looked down at their hands. No sparks had occurred this time, but she still felt electrified.

"Sasha Peters," he murmured softly. Her name sounded like the wind whispering through the pines. Gently he squeezed her fingers. "Someday you may be famous."

"That would sure surprise one person I know."

Jenny leaned toward her, puckering up her lips, and Sasha knew the child wanted a kiss. Leaning toward Jenny, her hand still held by Ross, Sasha touched her lips to the child's. Then she looked up.

Ross's fingers had tightened a little more around hers. Not enough to hurt, but enough to relay a message—the same message she saw in his eyes. What his daughter had wanted, he also wanted.

Her gaze touched his mouth. He did have a very nice mouth, his bottom lip sensuously full, a little dip breaking the straight line of his upper lip. She was certain his lips would feel good against hers. His kisses would be exciting. *Sasha Peters, what are you thinking?* she silently chided herself, and quickly slid her hand free from his and stepped back.

Ross cleared his throat. He'd seen a flicker of desire in her eyes, then surprise. He was also surprised. He wanted to kiss her, and if he didn't leave soon, he just might. "Well, I guess we'd better be going."

Outside, Nero and Polo, who'd been asleep on the patio, came to their feet and bounded over to greet the three of them. Looking for more cookies, they nuzzled Sasha's and Ross's hands. No longer afraid, Jenny leaned over in her father's arms and patted Nero's nose, then threw a kiss to Polo.

At the car Ross carefully buckled Jenny into her seat, closed the passenger door, then went around to his side. He paused before getting into the car and looked over the roof at Sasha. "Let me know when you get that contract."

"I will. I imagine it'll be sometime early next week. Are you still planning on coming to the story hour Wednesday?"

In the late-afternoon light with her face shadowed by the bonnet she'd put back on and the smooth lines of her dress enhancing her feminine curves, Sasha looked like a picture of a nineteenth-century country lady. A very lovely country lady, Ross decided. Soft. Feminine. Desirable. Yes, he'd be at Wednesday's story hour. "I wouldn't think of missing it."

"Good." She couldn't draw her eyes away from his face.

Finally Ross dropped his gaze. He wanted to ask her out, yet knew the idea was crazy. This was no time to get involved with a woman. He had his daughter to consider, his own life to get in order. Opening his car door, he called a final goodbye. "Well, until Wednesday, then."

"Until Wednesday."

She watched him turn his car around and drive up the steep hill to the main road. Almost as soon as the car disappeared from her view, a strange emptiness filled her. Quickly she picked up a stick and threw it for Nero to catch, certain that a bit of play with her dogs would fill the void she was experiencing. Both Nero and Polo went after the stick, with the bigger dog's three-leg handicap helping the little dog to keep up. But after a while Sasha realized that playing with her dogs was not going to take away the feeling of loneliness. Something was still missing.

A goat, she decided. It was time to buy the goat she wanted. Milking a goat, along with making her dolls and fixing the house, would keep her plenty busy. She wouldn't have time to be lonely, wouldn't have time to think about a man—about Ross Hammond. It didn't matter that her budget was strained to its limits. Soon she'd be signing a contract and have a lot of money. Sasha dropped the stick and went into the house to make a telephone call.

THE GOAT ARRIVED but not the contract. By Wednesday Sasha was getting worried. She was sure she hadn't imagined that call.

Ross brought Jenny to the story hour. At first the child stayed by his side, her Anna held close, but when Sasha brought out Mia, Jenny began to show more interest. And when Sasha asked Jenny to help tell the story of how Mia and Anna met, the little girl eagerly came over to sit beside her.

Ross was pleased. At the hospital, doctors had mended Jenny's broken body and therapists had taught her to walk again. Now Sasha was nurturing Jenny's independence.

When the hour was over and the others had left, Sasha told Ross she still hadn't received the contract. "Do you think they changed their minds?"

"Even if they use a standard form, business contracts take time to write and approve. Be patient."

So she was. She had to be. She had no other choice.

THE CONTRACT ARRIVED the following Tuesday. She spent the night reading it over, then rereading it, and was glad she'd hired a lawyer. As far as she was concerned, the entire document was purposely written to confuse.

On Wednesday, as soon as the mothers and children had left the library, she handed Ross the papers. Emma stood by the door, waiting for them to go so she could lock up. "I don't know what I'm giving them or not giving them. It's Greek to me."

"Why don't you let me read through it this afternoon while Jenny's taking a nap, then later we can go through it point by point. In fact, why don't you come to my place for dinner tonight? I'm no great cook, but I have learned how to boil spaghetti and heat up a jar of sauce." As irrational as it seemed, he'd been thinking more and more about asking her out. This seemed the perfect opportunity.

Sasha considered his invitation for a moment. She had planned on spending the entire afternoon and evening stripping the old wallpaper off the walls in the kitchen. Dinner with Ross and Jenny sounded a lot more enjoyable. "What time? And is there anything you'd like me to bring?"

"Just your smile."

SASHA BROUGHT MORE than her smile. She entered Ross's house carrying a hand puppet for Jenny and a sponge cake for Ross. "You didn't say anything about dessert. I thought if you fixed something, you and Jenny could always eat this later in the week."

"I bought ice cream. Your favorite." Suddenly he looked concerned. "You did tell Jenny that rocky road was your favorite. I hope you were serious."

He'd remembered. Sasha was pleased. "I was...I mean, it is. Thank you."

"Thank *you*. This looks good." Ross took the cake from her hands and set it on the table by the door, then reached out to help her with her coat. "Store-bought cakes are all we eat around here. I'm a rotten cook. My sister calls me a can-opener gourmet, but that's not really true." He chuckled. "Everything I cook doesn't come out

of a can. Most of the meals I fix come out of the freezer."
His hands rested on her shoulders for a second. "You
smell nice."

"Thank you." His touch was light, his fingertips barely
brushing her skin, and a whisper of excitement traveled
down her spine.

She wasn't entirely surprised by her reaction. She'd
been keyed up all afternoon, anticipating this visit. As
much as she tried to convince herself he'd only asked her
over because of the contract, that having dinner with
Ross in no way resembled a date, she knew that wasn't
so. Ross saw her as more than just a client; and to her
dismay, she couldn't seem to get him out of her own
thoughts.

Spending so much time thinking about a man wasn't
like her. Perhaps, she decided, she'd been isolating herself too much lately. She hadn't had a date since before
her sister's wedding. Somehow the wedding prepara-
tions, the move, redoing her house and her regular work
had kept her too busy to think about going out. That,
plus the lack of anyone in the area who interested her.

Ross Hammond, however, did interest her. Too much.

As soon as her coat was off, she moved away from him
and looked around his house. "I like what you've done.
I was here once before when Mrs. Williams was still alive.
She kept the shades drawn, and the place seemed so dark.
Now it has an open, airy feel."

She could see into the living-room and dining areas.
Thelma Williams's heavy, dark antique furnishings, lace
doilies and myriad knickknacks had been replaced with
contemporary pieces of furniture—functional, taste-
fully designed and very expensive looking. The house's
decor reminded her of Ross. His clothing also projected
a feeling of good taste and quality. Only once had she

seen him in a sweatshirt and jeans. Normally he wore slacks, a shirt and either a cable-knit sweater or a sport jacket. This evening was no exception. He was model perfect in a brown tweed sport coat, gold shirt and brown slacks and shoes. She had to admit the man looked good.

He also smelled good. When he'd helped her with her coat, the scent of his after-shave had surrounded her. But now another odor reached her nostrils. She sniffed and wrinkled up her nose. "Do I smell something burning?"

"Oh, damn! The beans!" Quickly hanging Sasha's coat on a hook by the door, Ross hurried by her into the kitchen.

She followed, entering the room just as he stuck a smoking pan under the faucet and turned on the water. Steam billowed toward the ceiling, and the smell of burned green beans filled the air.

"I thought I had enough water in them," he said apologetically. "I'm afraid they're ruined."

From the smell and the look of the blackened pan, Sasha had to agree.

Jenny entered the kitchen at that moment. As soon as she saw Sasha, she grinned and headed straight for her.

"Hi, sweetheart." Squatting, Sasha embraced and picked up the small child.

Ross opened the window over the sink to let the room air out. "She's been playing in her bedroom. I don't think she heard the doorbell when you arrived. Otherwise, she would have been at the door with me." Scorched pan in hand, he headed for the back door. "She's been excited all afternoon about your coming here . . . wanted to get dressed up as soon as she woke from her nap. Excuse me for a minute. I'm going to dump these outside."

He went out and Sasha held Jenny back a bit to look at the child's white dress decorated with little red hearts.

"You look very pretty tonight. See what I brought you?"
Sasha showed her the hand puppet. "Put out your hand,
and I'll show you how it works."

Obediently Jenny put out her hand, and Sasha slipped
the cloth body over her small fingers while the puppet's
papier-mâché head bobbed until Jenny's middle finger
slipped into place.

Ross came back into the kitchen carrying the empty
pan, then stopped as the outside door closed with a click
behind him. Jenny looked so happy, her blue eyes bright
with delight, her little mouth forming silent laughter
when the puppet on her hand bowed and wiggled. Such
a simple toy, yet so perfect for a young child. He admired Sasha's knack for knowing what would please his
daughter.

For a second he simply stood and stared. Sasha looked
absolutely gorgeous, her pale blond curls softly framing
her face, the dark green color of her wool dress bringing
out the green of her eyes. Jenny momentarily let the hand
puppet rest against Sasha's chest, and Ross found himself wishing it were his hand holding the puppet. A
tightening in his loins betrayed the direction of his
thoughts, and he quickly turned and headed for the sink.

Sasha Peters was doing it to him again, arousing a desire he'd thought he'd forgotten, or at least had more
control over. He'd have to remember never to wear tight-
fitting slacks around her. Turning on the hot water, he
filled the scorched pan. "I'm afraid we go without a veg-
etable tonight."

"Do you have any lettuce?" Sasha asked, giving Jenny
a loving squeeze before putting the child down.

"I think so."

She brushed the wrinkles out of her long skirt, then
moved toward him. "How 'bout if I make a salad?"

"Good idea." He should have thought of it himself. His mind seemed to be on matters other than food.

Sasha found lettuce in the refrigerator and a can of mixed vegetables in the cupboard. She passed up jars of commercial salad dressing to mix her own vinegar-and-oil combination. A few minutes later she carried the finished salad into the dining room.

There she had to smile. It looked as though a child had set the table, the forks reversed with the knives and spoons, napkins plopped on the plates. "Did Jenny help you with the table?" she called back into the kitchen.

Ross was draining the spaghetti into a colander. He leaned back to avoid the steam. "No, I set it myself. Why?"

Her smile grew wider. "No reason. Did you have a chance to look at that contract?"

"I did." He glanced over his shoulder and found her leaning against the doorjamb. "Let's wait until after dinner to discuss it."

"That bad?"

He dumped the spaghetti onto a large platter. "Let's say you made the right decision in consulting a lawyer."

IT WAS AFTER seven o'clock by the time they'd finished dinner and cleared the table. The spaghetti had long passed the al dente stage, nearly disintegrating on a fork, but the sauce had tasted good. Ross had ruefully pointed out that all he'd had to do with that was open a jar and heat it. "But I guess I am getting better. At least I didn't burn it."

He grinned, and Sasha liked the boyish appeal his features took on when the corners of his mouth turned up. She also liked the fact that he was smiling more often.

The rocky road ice cream went perfectly with the cake. After they did the dishes, they got Jenny ready for bed. Sasha was easily talked into telling a bedtime story using the hand puppet. Jenny was asleep before they left the room.

"The contract's in my office," Ross said, casually touching the small of her back as they went down the stairs. "Why don't you go on in and sit down while I get us something to drink. Brandy all right?"

"Actually I'm not much of a drinker, but I could go for another cup of tea." The wine she'd had with dinner was more than she was used to, and she'd felt a little fuzzy while doing the dishes with Ross by her side. That had bothered her. Now she felt light-headed again—just from a simple touch of his hand. This wouldn't do. She was here on business. At least, that was what she kept telling herself.

"One brandy and one tea coming up," he agreed. "Make yourself at home."

He left her in his newly revamped office, and Sasha wandered around the room. As far as she could remember, it had been a sitting room when Thelma Williams owned the house. Ross had made a lot of changes, the most noticeable being the bookshelves that covered two walls. Impressive tomes now resided on those shelves, and she wondered if Ross had read all of them and could quote decisions, as she'd seen lawyers on television do.

Beside a paneled window was a large oak desk with a leather chair behind it and two upholstered chairs in front. Her contract was lying on top of the desk. She walked over and picked it up. He'd stuck some yellow Post-its on the paper, with a sentence or two on each. She tried to read one and found his handwriting indecipherable.

"If you can read that, you're better than most. My secretary always said I should have been a doctor," Ross stated, coming up next to her. He handed her a mug of tea and held a snifter of brandy for himself. "Shall we get started?"

"Fine with me."

Sasha sat in one of the upholstered chairs, and Ross pulled the other up beside her. Sentence by sentence they went through the contract. After reading it over once, he took off his tweed jacket, rolled up his shirtsleeves and got a refill of brandy while she made more tea. Then they read through the contract again. This time Ross explained what each section meant to her personally, asked for her ideas, and suggested changes.

She was impressed with his thoroughness. From artistic control to percentages of profit, anything that was not in her favor was revised. After the third time through, Ross laid the contract on his desk, then sat back in his chair and flexed his shoulders. "That should do it."

"Do you really think they'll go for all those changes?"

"Not all of them, but you won't get anything if you don't ask for it."

"So, what do I do next?" She hated the idea of telling Mr. Bernstein she wasn't going to sign what he'd sent.

"*You* do nothing. Now is when your lawyer calls their lawyer."

Her lawyer. She liked the sound of that. It made her feel more secure. There could be a problem, however. Foolishly she'd gone and spent most of her extra cash on a goat, and she doubted if Ross would take goat's milk in exchange for his services. "We never did discuss how much you charge. I have a twenty with me."

She reached into the pocket of her dress, but he placed a hand on her sleeve, stopping her from drawing out the money. "You don't have to pay me anything tonight, Sasha. In fact, you don't have to pay me anything until you're satisfied with this contract, it's been signed and you've been paid by the company."

His attitude surprised her. She'd expected a lawyer—especially a city lawyer—to be a stickler on money matters. "But what if Benson Toys doesn't agree to the changes we've made? What if I don't ever sign the contract?"

"Then I get nothing." It was as simple as that to him. He didn't need her money. He had enough invested to get by for the rest of his life.

"That doesn't sound like something a man bent on success would say."

"Ah, but remember—I've changed. I've learned there are some things in life that are more important than money and success."

She remembered. She also knew having him go over the contract and explain it to her was worth something. "I insist on paying you, whether I sign or not."

He smiled. Around Sasha he was finding it easier to smile. "You could give me a small token of your appreciation."

He knew what he wanted—and it wasn't money. For too many nights he'd lain awake wondering how her lips would taste. His eyes drifted to them. She'd eaten off her lipstick, but her mouth looked delicious. Absolutely delicious.

Sasha felt a lovely warmth surge through her arteries. "A token . . . of my appreciation," she said, her voice cracking midsentence.

"Only if you're willing." He leaned toward her, his fingers tightening slightly on her arm, only inches separating their faces. "Sasha?"

"Yes?" She knew what he was asking.

"Will you kiss me?"

4

GAZING INTO THE BLUE depths of his eyes, Sasha whispered "Yes," and the space between them was closed.

Ross's mouth totally covered hers, his lips firm yet soft, demanding while giving. He'd asked for a token of her appreciation. Well, she did appreciate his help, his sincerity and his warmth. One kiss became many. He maintained his grip on her arm and touched her opposite shoulder with his other hand, turning her even more toward him. Slanting his head, he tried new angles, kissed the corners of her mouth, pulled on her lower lip, then let it go. And to every kiss she responded.

It seemed right, natural, and so very wonderful. Without even thinking about it, her hand went to his shirtsleeve so that her fingers rested over a well-developed but not overly large biceps. She could feel the muscle ripple when his hand moved to her cheek. He combed his fingers through her tight curls and played with the pearl stud in her earlobe. Then slowly, as though caressing silk, he let his fingertips travel down her neck to her shoulder again.

Tingles of pleasure coursed through her body. Stunned, Sasha pulled back. Her heartbeat erratic, she stared at Ross. She'd suspected he might try to kiss her before the evening ended, but she hadn't thought she'd enjoy it this much.

"I have a confession to make," he murmured, his gaze devouring her.

"What's that?" She let go of his arm.

"I've wanted to kiss you ever since you walked into the house tonight."

"And now that you have?"

He smiled. Not in mockery, but seductively. Placing his hand behind her head, he drew her face back toward his and softly gave his answer. "I want to kiss you again."

Her lips were as pure and as delicious as honey. He couldn't seem to get enough. Desire, not curiosity, now motivated his actions. He ran the tip of his tongue over her lips, and she automatically opened her mouth, inviting him in. Eagerly he accepted the invitation.

Eyes closed, she felt the steady, firm thrust of his tongue. She could taste the brandy he'd been drinking, feel the need he was expressing. It was easy for her to imagine another part of his body entering her. Immediately muscles between her legs contracted in anticipation.

Sasha held her breath, disconcerted by the physical desire she was experiencing. It had been a while since a kiss had gotten her this aroused. A long while since any man had interested her as Ross did. She exhaled shakily.

The sound of her ragged breath made Ross pull back. Flaxen lashes lay on rosy cheeks, then lifted slowly to reveal the gold-flecked green of her eyes. She looked dazed, and he was glad. He felt dazed, confused. This wasn't the time to get involved with a woman, yet he didn't seem to have any control over the matter. Mentally Sasha Peters fascinated him, emotionally she soothed him and physically...

His body ached for release, and from the way Sasha was responding, he didn't think she'd be entirely opposed to the idea of making love. Yet he had a feeling that if they did, they would both regret their actions afterward. Whatever tenuous relationship they now shared would die, and he didn't want that to happen.

With his hand trembling slightly, he brushed the backs of his fingers over her cheek. "Wow!"

"Wow is right," she agreed, her own voice none too steady.

His fingers slid over her jaw to the graceful line of her neck. Feeling the rapid beat of her pulse against his knuckles, he smiled. "Nothing like a little lovemaking to get the heart pumping."

"Ross, I don't . . . That is, I—"

"Shh." He leaned forward and silenced her with a kiss. "Don't worry," he murmured over her lips. "We're not going to rush into anything."

More kisses, mingled with words of assurance, kept her objections at bay. Then his hand moved from her throat to cover one breast, and total confusion washed over her. She liked the feel of his hand, the erotic way his fingertips caressed the turgid peak of her nipple, circled wider, then came back to home in on that very sensitive point. A quivering longing spiraled through her, the heat of passion flowing along her arteries.

He said they weren't going to rush into anything, but things were going much too fast for her. Covering his hand with hers, she pushed his fingers away. "Ross, don't . . . please."

"Sasha?" He drew his head back slightly to study her flushed face. "Does my touching you there bother you?"

"Yes . . . no." She looked down, avoiding his penetrating eyes. How could she answer such a question?

Gently he tilted her head up. "I want to touch all of you."

"Ross, you said we weren't going to rush into anything."

For a moment he said nothing. His physical needs were warring with reason. Then, with a sigh of frustration, he released his hold and sat back in his chair. "So I did."

Sasha also sat back. Now that he'd drawn away from her, she felt an emptiness.

"What a dilemma." He scoffed at the situation. "Here I am, a man, thirty-three years old, healthy in all ways and sitting next to one of the loveliest women I've ever met. Every instinct tells me to make love to you, to—"

She started to object, but he again turned toward her, holding up a hand. "Let me finish. Okay?"

Sasha stifled her argument.

"My problem is, I'm a man who also has a four-year-old daughter upstairs. A daughter who can't talk, who needs my care. The doctors say her vocal cords are all right, that they've just been traumatized. They say the problem's more emotional—psychological—than physical, and in time she'll talk again. But they don't give any guarantees or dates. It could be tomorrow. It could be years from now."

"You'll just have to be patient." It seemed an empty statement, but she didn't know what else to say.

"Patience, I think, is the hardest thing I'm having to learn. The doctors tell me to be patient. My family tells me to be patient...." He sighed. "If I were a patient man, Sasha, I'd have waited before kissing you, waited until I knew what direction my life was taking. But no. I wanted to kiss you, so I did. And now what? I can't wine and dine you, can't invite you to exciting places or dance the night away. I have my child to take care of. I failed her for three and a half years of her life. I can't fail her again."

"You won't," she assured him. Reaching over the arms of the two chairs, Sasha took his hand in hers and gave it a squeeze. "I don't want to be wined and dined or in-

vited to exciting places. And I'm really not that great a
dancer. I know you have responsibilities. And you're
doing a good job...a great job, Ross. Jenny already looks
better than when I first saw her. Healthier. Happier."

He looked at the slender fingers on his, then at her.
"Still, I'm attracted to you. You know that, don't you?"

She nodded.

"And I think you're attracted to me."

It wasn't something she could deny—not after the kiss
they'd just shared.

"So what do we do?" he asked.

"Can't we simply be friends?"

"'Friends'?"

She grinned at the surprise she heard in his voice. "Yes,
friends."

He wanted to be her lover but knew she was right.
Until Jenny was better, a friendship was all he could of-
fer. Patting the hand on his, he leaned back in his chair.
"So, my friend, tell me all about yourself."

"What do you want to know?" There was much of her
past she wouldn't share, not even with a friend.

"Tell me what you were like as a child. When you
started making dolls? Telling stories to children?"

Those questions she could answer—at least in part.
"As a child I was a dreamer, or so my father always said.
I don't really remember when I started making dolls. I
used to make them out of anything I found around the
house. I first came up with the idea for the My Friends
dolls after my mother read *Little Women* to my sister and
me. I created the first one when I was ten."

"Your sister's older or younger?" Ross interrupted.

"Older, by two years."

"Any other brothers or sisters?"

"No, after I was born, Mom couldn't have any more children." Sasha sometimes wondered if her mother could have had more, if things had been different. If there'd been other children, maybe her father wouldn't have picked on her so. She would never know. "What about you? You said you have a sister, the one who bought Anna for Jenny. Do you have more than one? Any brothers?"

"No. One boy, one girl. That was all my folks wanted. Nowadays my parents would be called Yuppies. They'd grown up during World War II and had to do without. They wanted their children to have the best of everything and felt they could only offer that by limiting the size of their family. I'm afraid, much as I love them, that they stressed material possessions too much. It's taken me quite awhile to discover money doesn't buy happiness."

From what he'd told her, it had taken the car accident. "And your sister? Does she stress material possessions?"

"Not like our parents. Ann does work hard—she's a real-estate broker and a very successful one, at that—but her work isn't everything to her." Not as it had been to him. "She knows how to enjoy life, relax and have fun. One of these days she'll be up here for a visit. I'd like you to meet her."

"That would be nice." If Ann Hammond was anything like her brother, Sasha was certain she'd like the woman. "I'm sure you'll be meeting my sister sometime soon. In a town as small as Putnam, paths cross. In fact, maybe I should introduce you to her. Tanya might be able to help you with Jenny. She minored in child psychology in college and is very good with young children."

Leaning across the arms of the two chairs, Ross kissed her cheek. "So are you."

His lips were warm, but a shiver ran down Sasha's spine. They'd agreed to be friends, yet one simple kiss from him had her on edge, wanting more. Letting go of his hand, she stood. "I think I'd better be on my way home. It's getting late."

A clock on the wall verified her statement. Ross also stood. "Want what's left of your cake back?"

"Oh, no. You two eat that. You can bring me the plate next Wednesday."

At the door he helped her with her coat, then turned her so she was facing him. With his hands on her shoulders and only inches separating them, he looked down into her eyes. "I enjoy your company, Sasha," he told her honestly. "You're easy to talk to, comfortable to be around."

"I'm glad. I enjoy your company, too." There was a husky rasp in her voice that emphasized the effect his company was having on her.

His fingers tightened on her shoulders, and he drew her closer.

"Ross?"

"Yes," he answered above her mouth.

"Friends . . . Remember?"

"Friends kiss."

His lips touched hers, and she couldn't say anything more. Not that she wanted to say anything more. Kissing Ross was too delightful to ruin with conversation. Too pleasurable. Too mind-boggling. Friends did kiss, but not this way.

Although their clothing formed a barrier and dulled sensation, the feeling of her soft breasts against his chest was arousingly tempting. His arms moved from her shoulders to encircle her back, and he squeezed a little, increasing the contact. The feeling was good, his body automatically reacting, and he drew in a ragged breath. His lungs couldn't seem to get enough air. Pressing his face against her curls, he held her close and tried breathing deeply. He needed to keep control. Then he chuckled as he realized each time he inhaled he was pushing his chest against hers. "Lady, you feel good. Damn good."

She might have said the same about him, but she didn't trust her voice. She was glad he was holding her tightly. Her legs felt so wobbly, she was afraid that if he let her go, she'd collapse at his feet.

"Remember that first day we met, when I went to take Jenny and ended up with my hands on you?"

She remembered. "Yes."

"I didn't know what to say. I felt I should apologize, but the truth was, I enjoyed every second." He moved one hand around to her side. Shifting his position slightly, he let his fingers cover Sasha's breast. "I don't think I've ever touched a woman who feels as good as you do."

"Ross..." she groaned, her knees growing even weaker as his hand stimulated an already taut nipple.

"I'll stop if you really want me to," he promised, but continued stroking. "You just feel so good to me."

His touch felt good to her, too. Too good to stop. Confused by her own need, Sasha closed her eyes. As his hand caressed, his lips teased her face, making a trail from one cheek across the bridge of her nose to her other cheek. Finally he kissed her mouth, and Sasha felt her insides turn to molten lava. His tongue slid past her teeth to stroke the sensitive interior of her mouth.

Boldly she accepted him, her tongue parrying with his until the room seemed to spin and she could scarcely breathe. "Ross, please," she begged, pulling her head back and panting for air. It was an earnest plea, but she wasn't sure what she wanted him to do—stop or go further.

He knew what he had to do. To continue as he was, his body aching to know her, would be pure folly. He stopped the kisses and caresses.

Without words he held her close, stared over her head at a knothole on his door and tried to make some sense out of his feelings. He could feel her rapid heartbeat and smiled. Sasha Peters might be called the Doll Lady, but she was no inanimate toy. The woman in his arms was vibrantly alive and possessed a passionate nature he wanted to know better. Before he released his hold, he whispered into her hair, "When can I see you again?"

Shaken, she answered cautiously. "I suppose next Wednesday.... If you bring Jenny to the story hour."

He leaned back slightly so he could see her face. "Sasha, I want to see you before then."

She wasn't sure that that was a good idea. They'd agreed to be friends; friendship was a nice, safe relationship. The way he'd kissed her tonight, the way she'd responded ... She needed time to think. "I'm going to be very busy this week. I'm stripping the wallpaper in the kitchen, then I'm going to start work on that porch. I've got doll orders to fill and—"

"You're looking for excuses."

And he wasn't buying them. "Ross, I'm really quite happy with my life as it is. I'm not sure I want to complicate it. You've already said Jenny needs you. I think it would be best if we didn't see each other—-that is, other than when you bring her to my story hour or when we just happen to run into each other."

He had no intention of ignoring his daughter, but he also had no intention of limiting his contact with Sasha to chance meetings. "Like it or not, you've complicated my life. I think it only fair that I complicate yours. Have dinner with me Friday night. Here. Nothing fancy. I can order a pizza or something. Jenny would love it. I would love it."

"No," Sasha insisted. "This is a small town. I'm sure your neighbors already know I'm here tonight. If I come Friday night, people will have us paired up before you know it."

"And that's so bad?"

She forced herself to step back, away from the support of his arms. "Not bad...not good. Ross, I don't want to get involved."

"We are involved."

She shook her head. "You're wrong. I need you as a lawyer and I'll be your friend, but if you want more, I suggest you find another woman."

"I don't want another woman." He knew that for certain now. It wasn't just a physical release he was looking for; it was Sasha who interested him, and no one else.

"I treasure my independence."

"You can still have it."

She scoffed. "That I doubt."

"Give us a chance."

"I need time to think."

Maybe she was right about that; maybe they both needed time to think. Patience wasn't his forte, but it looked as though life were giving him a few lessons in the art. "All right. You spend the next few days thinking, and Jenny and I'll take you to lunch after your story hour Wednesday."

"Ross—" She started to object.

"That is, if you're free after your story hour," he quickly added. "I don't want to interfere with your independence."

"Now you're making fun of me."

"No, I'm not."

His serious tone said he wasn't. She sighed. "We'll see."

It was better than a definite rejection. "Until Wednesday, then."

"Until Wednesday," she agreed and turned toward the door.

Quickly he stepped over to open it. "Also, thanks again for the cake . . . and for bringing Jenny that puppet. I'll get in touch with Benson Toys tomorrow morning. Don't be surprised if you get a call from them. Just don't let them intimidate you, Sasha. Remember, they want what's best for them and won't give you anything you don't ask for."

"I'm not easily intimidated."

"No, I don't imagine you are." As delicate as she appeared, he'd already discovered she had a stubborn streak. Though it was proving frustrating, he admired her tenacity.

With the door open, the cold night air flowed into the house, and Sasha pulled her coat tightly around her. Clouds covered the moon and the stars, but a streetlight illuminated Ross's yard. Her Chevy, its gray finish dulled from years of exposure to sunshine and harsh weather, was parked in his driveway. She stepped out onto the porch.

"Drive carefully going home. Okay?" Ross called after her.

Sasha laughed lightly. "I only have to go a couple of miles."

"Maybe so, but part of the way's practically straight down, and that car of yours doesn't look very reliable."

"It may be old, but the brakes are good and it gets me places."

"Still . . ." He glanced over his shoulder, up the stairs that went to his daughter's room. "If it weren't for Jenny, I'd follow you home."

She frowned. "Ross Hammond, I'm quite capable of taking care of myself. I don't need a protector."

He forced himself to say nothing. She'd obviously been taking care of herself for several years. Yet the idea of her driving home alone late at night concerned him. "Call me when you get home."

"All right, I'll call you," she said, lifting the hem of her dress as she went down the steps. At her car she looked back. "See you Wednesday."

"Wednesday," he repeated. He wondered how he could go an entire week without seeing her again.

SHE CALLED AS SOON as she got home, and somehow they ended up talking for another hour, about nothing in particular and about everything, until Sasha could barely keep her eyes open and had to hang up. It rained all day Thursday and most of Friday, which was fine with her, since California needed the water and since the only time she had to go outside was to milk the goat. Otherwise, she spent the two days working on doll orders and the evenings soaking and scraping layer upon layer of old wallpaper off her kitchen walls. Contrary to Ross's warning, no one from Benson Toys called. She wasn't sure if that was good or bad. There was the possibility that the company wasn't all that interested in her doll design and that when Ross called about making changes in the contract, they'd told him to forget the whole idea.

Twice she almost called him to find out what Benson Toys had said, then stopped herself. She knew what would happen if she did. They'd talk, he'd ask her out and she'd have a dilemma. She needed Ross's expertise as a lawyer and knew that living in a small community they'd see each other often, so logically a friendship was all they should share. No dates. No kisses. No touching. And certainly no lovemaking.

But logic didn't govern the needs of her body. Darn it all. If she could simply enjoy sex as sex, without getting emotionally involved, there'd be no problem. But that wasn't her nature. She couldn't give her body without truly caring for a man. And she knew from past experience that when she got involved with a man, he became very proprietary.

Never again would she let someone tell her who she was. Never. Her relationship with Ross had to remain platonic.

Saturday the sun came out. With her doll orders up-to-date, Sasha decided it was a perfect day to spend outside, tearing down the old porch. Rising early, as usual, she put on one of her older dresses, milked the goat, fed the animals and herself, then started to work. It was close to ten o'clock when Nero and Polo lifted their heads from the ground near her feet, then jumped up barking. Putting down the crowbar, Sasha stepped back from the porch to see who was coming.

The moment she recognized Ross's BMW, her heart rate doubled and butterflies took flight in her stomach. Wiping her palms on her long skirt, she licked her lips and wondered how she looked.

Ross thought she looked wonderful standing next to the sagging porch, the sunlight turning her short curls into tight coils of white gold and bringing out the healthy glow of her skin. He also hoped she could stem the silent tears streaming down his daughter's cheeks. Ignoring the barking dogs, as soon as he'd parked he hurried around the car to get Jenny out.

"We have an emergency," he called, cradling Jenny on one hip and holding Anna out toward Sasha. "I don't know how it happened. There must have been a nail that wasn't all the way in. Jenny was playing on the stairs and snagged Anna's arm. I can't get her to stop crying."

Sasha met them halfway, and Ross handed her the doll. "Can it be fixed?"

She looked at the ragged tear just below Anna's left elbow, where a bit of stuffing poked out. Then she looked at Jenny. The child wasn't making a sound, but her cheeks were wet, and her eyes glistened with tears. Sorrow needed no voice.

"Of course we can fix it," she assured father and child. "Let's take Anna inside."

In the living room, after washing her hands, Sasha picked up her sewing bag and sat down on the sofa. "Put Jenny here, next to me, so she can watch what I do," she directed Ross, indicating a spot on her left side. "We'll have Anna fixed up in no time."

He placed his daughter next to Sasha, then stepped back to stand near the fireplace. From there he watched Sasha match a thread to the natural-colored felt of the doll's arm. Quickly a needle was threaded, the ragged edges of the torn felt were neatly trimmed and the stuffing was pushed back into the hole. Then, using very small, tight slipstitches, Sasha began to close the opening. And all the while she worked, Sasha talked to Jenny, assuring the little girl that all active children got hurt from time to time and saying she'd bet Jenny had gotten cuts and scrapes more than once.

Jenny nodded. Her tears had dried, and she was watching the operation intently.

Within minutes the hole was closed and the thread had been secured and snipped clean. Only a faint line remained, barely noticeable. Satisfied with the results, Sasha handed the doll back to Jenny. "There she is, as good as new. Just tell your daddy to fix that nail so Anna doesn't get hurt again."

Jenny looked over at Ross, her blue eyes now sparkling with pleasure.

"I'll take care of it as soon as we get back to the house," he promised.

He wasn't in a big hurry to leave, however. Since Wednesday night he'd wanted to see Sasha again, and that morning he'd actually been trying to think of an excuse to drive out to her place. Now that he was here, he intended to stay for a while. "Did you get a call from Benson Toys?"

"No. Should I have?" she asked, concerned. Perhaps she shouldn't have hesitated to call Ross. Maybe there had been problems.

"Not necessarily. I talked to your Mr. Bernstein Thursday morning, then to their contract lawyer. I think Bernstein was surprised you'd gone to a lawyer."

"Did he sound upset?" She didn't want to be unreasonable in her demands, yet she also wanted to protect herself.

"Guarded would better describe his reaction." Ross watched Jenny climb off the sofa, tuck Anna under one arm and head straight for the dolls leaning against the steamer chest on the floor. "Jenny, don't touch anything you shouldn't," he warned.

Sasha saw where the child was going. "She's welcome to play with the dolls. That's what they're for. Would you like something to drink? Some instant coffee?" She put her sewing materials away, then stood.

"A cup of coffee sounds good." It meant she wanted him to stay, at least for a while longer.

In the kitchen he immediately noticed the stripped walls. "You've been busy."

"The messy part's done. Now I've got to wait until I can afford to buy the paper. Money... I never seem to have enough." She put on the teakettle and nodded in the direction of the porch, where she'd been working when he arrived. "Out there I'm going to have to replace all the boards. I'd hoped to save some, but they're all rotted. I can tear them off now and make it safer for kids to be around, but I can't afford the lumber until either that contract is signed and Benson Toys pays me or I sell a lot more dolls. Sometimes I think my father was right."

"How's that?" asked Ross, leaning back against the counter to watch as she got two cups and saucers down from the cupboard, spoons from a drawer and instant coffee from the refrigerator. He'd never thought of keeping coffee in the refrigerator. He preferred perked, anyway, but his was usually so strong that it was bitter.

"Oh, Dad always said I should go to college, that someday I would regret not having a good education and a steady job. Times like now make me wonder if he was right."

"Sign that contract and you'll be paid well. You didn't go to college, then?" Once, that might have mattered to him. Before, when he'd been single, he'd equated educational level with social status and had felt, for his career, that he had to limit his choices of women to those who could help him move forward and upward. Donna had had that college diploma, had fit his criteria to a T. Now none of that mattered.

"As soon as I graduated from high school, I moved out on my own and started making dolls." Sasha laughed a little, recalling those days. "I don't know why a lack of money bothers me now. I was really living from hand to mouth then."

"It was rough?" He wondered about her parents' finances. "What's your father do?"

"Dad's a salesman for a food-packaging company, but I didn't want any money from him." Not that he would have given her any. "I wanted to make it on my own." To show him. "So besides making dolls, I had to take a job waiting tables. I hated that, and as soon as I had enough boutiques selling my dolls, and enough special orders, I quit."

"And did you wait tables in your long dresses?" His gaze moved down over the pink-and-white checked one she had on. The sleeves were frayed at the elbows, and the garment looked as though it had seen several seasons of wear.

"Yes, as a matter of fact I did. The restaurant was called Granny's Pantry, and all the waitresses wore long, old-fashioned dresses like this. In fact, because I had to go to work right after I finished, I had one of the dresses on the first time I put on a puppet show. I received so many compliments on my costume that I decided dressing like my dolls might be a good promotional gimmick. So I made a few long dresses to match the ones my dolls wore and started wearing them whenever I visited boutiques or presented a puppet show. After a while I was wearing them all the time."

From her jar of tea leaves, she filled a tea ball and set it in a small porcelain pot. "People have become so accustomed to seeing me in a long dress that I think if I walked down the streets of Putnam in shorts, I'd shock everyone."

"You wouldn't shock me. I'd like to see you in shorts." He stared at her floor-length skirt. The unknown was always tempting. In his fantasies he'd imagined her in shorts, in a bikini and without any clothes on. Someday, he hoped, fantasy would become reality.

"Well, don't hold your breathe. My legs aren't that great to look at. Besides, I'm so darn top-heavy that a long skirt helps balance me out."

His eyes moved up to the full curves of her breasts. "You've got a great figure."

She laughed at the comment. "Most men think so, but believe me, having large breasts isn't all that great. You should try finding ready-made clothes that will fit."

The kettle whistled and she went to the stove. "For some reason, commercial dress designers believe if you have a 42-inch bust, you must therefore have 42-inch hips. I've had to make my own clothes for years." She poured some water into the teapot, then motioned for him to come over. "I'll let you fix your own coffee. Then if it's too strong or too weak, you'll have to blame yourself."

Ross moved to her side, chuckling. "You complain about too much. My mother and sister always complain about too little." He looked directly at her breasts, then at her face. "Have you ever thought of having breast reduction?"

Her gaze met his. "No. Much as I gripe, they're a part of me."

"Good." Sliding an arm around her shoulders, he drew her close and gave her an affectionate squeeze. "Because I think you have a lovely figure . . . and an equally lovely mouth." Which he kissed.

The two days he'd spent without her had seemed an eternity. He'd never considered himself a man who couldn't live without a woman, was still sure he was in total control of his emotions, but he had to admit—if only to himself—that he felt more alive whenever he was around Sasha.

His kiss caught her by surprise. She'd made up her mind that they shouldn't kiss again, but the moment his lips touched hers, she forgot that resolution. Her heart rate doubled, and the day seemed brighter than before. Willingly she responded to the pressure of his mouth.

How long the kiss might have lasted or how far it might have taken them, neither would know. As Ross brought her closer and Sasha rose on her toes, Nero and Polo began barking. Their excited warning meant only one thing. Someone was coming.

Sasha pulled back, and Ross let her go. They both looked out the kitchen window and saw the white pickup truck pull into the yard and park next to Ross's car. Her cheeks still flushed, Sasha smiled. "It's my sister."

5

AT THE DOG'S BARKING, Jenny, clutching Anna, ran into the kitchen. Ross scooped up child and doll and carried the pair outside to meet the slender strawberry-blonde who stepped out of the white truck. Jenny buried her face against his neck when Sasha introduced them to her sister.

Tanya's figure wasn't quite as voluptuous as Sasha's. She was a bit taller, with long straight hair that was a much darker, redder shade of blond than Sasha's, and her eyes were blue instead of green. Nevertheless, there was a strong family resemblance between the sisters.

"He's my lawyer," Sasha told Tanya, hoping her recently kissed lips wouldn't give away the other side of her relationship with Ross. "He went over the contract Benson Toys sent. And thank goodness he did. The way they had it written, if I'd signed, I couldn't have said anything, no matter what they decided to do with the dolls."

Tanya's eyes moved from Sasha's flushed face to Ross. She smiled knowingly, and proudly slung an arm around Sasha's shoulders. "What do you think of this sister of mine? I'll be able to say I knew her when."

"That is if Benson Toys agrees to the changes we made in the contract." Sasha didn't feel all that confident the company would.

"They'll make the changes. Maybe not all we asked for, but I think they'll go with most," Ross insisted. His gaze switched from Sasha to Tanya. "To answer your question, I think your sister's pretty fantastic."

Tanya's smile turned to a wide grin. "So do I. And I think maybe a lawyer is just what we've needed around here."

Jenny dared a peek at the woman standing in front of her father.

"Hi," Tanya greeted, putting out a hand to touch Jenny's small arm.

Immediately Jenny pulled her arm away and under her body and hid her face back against Ross's shoulder.

"I'm afraid she's become very shy around strangers," he apologized.

"No problem. In time she'll get to know I don't bite."

"Ha, that's what she says," scoffed Sasha. "I remember when we were growing up. She bit me more than once."

"Because you always pulled my hair." Tanya winked at Ross. "Of course, that might have been because I used to threaten to tell Dad she was making dolls."

"Your dad didn't want you making dolls?" Ross asked Sasha. The idea surprised him.

"My father and I look at life in different ways," Sasha answered, then quickly turned to Tanya. "Ross and I were just fixing ourselves something to drink. Come on in. The tea should be ready."

The subject had been changed. Quite abruptly, Ross noted. He watched Sasha lead the way back into the house, then followed.

By the stove he made his coffee, hampered somewhat by Jenny, who now refused to leave his arms. And while he mixed and stirred, Sasha got another cup and saucer down for her sister and poured tea for the two of them. For Jenny Sasha got a glass of milk—goat's milk. But when the child spat out the first taste, it was exchanged for orange juice.

They sat around the butcher-block table, with Jenny on Ross's lap and Anna draped over her legs. For a long time the little girl simply sipped her juice and listened as the adults talked. Finally, when her glass was empty, Jenny ventured off her father's lap. Standing beside him, she began pulling on his leg and pointing into the other room.

"What do you want?" he asked, uncertain how to read his daughter's gestures.

Shifting her weight from leg to leg, Jenny continued trying to relay her message, then lifted Anna's gingham dress and pulled on the doll's panties.

"Ah." Ross finally understood. "Where is your bathroom?" he asked Sasha, his cheeks turning pink. There were many aspects of being a little girl's father and sole parent that he wasn't used to yet.

"It's just off the living room, to the right," she directed.

When Ross came back into the kitchen, he was alone. "She decided to stay and play with the dolls by the trunk."

"She doesn't talk at all?" asked Tanya.

"No. Not at all," Ross answered.

"Doesn't make any noises? Not even in her sleep?"

"None that I've heard. I thought she gave a small cry the first time I came out here." He glanced at Sasha. "But I guess I was mistaken."

"If she did, I didn't hear it." Sasha wished she could say she had. She knew how much Jenny's silence bothered him.

Tanya looked pensive. "Have you considered teaching her sign language?"

"The doctors said not to, at least not yet. They want me to encourage her to talk." He shrugged. "But then they also said not to pressure her, that she's going to need time to adjust to everything that's happened to her. You've both seen how shy she is when she meets someone new, how she clings to me. Actually she's better now. For a while I felt like I was being smothered. She was so afraid I was going to disappear, she wouldn't let me out of her sight. At least now she's beginning to play by herself."

He pointed toward the living room. "That she's in there and we're in here is a big step for her. A month ago she wouldn't have left my side for anything."

"Is she around other children at all?"

"I've been taking her to Sasha's story hour on Wednesdays. I've seen a big improvement there. At first I had to be right by her side. Now she'll sit with the other children."

"Good." Tanya nodded her approval. "Encourage her to play with children her age as much as possible. Do you talk to Jenny about what happened?"

"No." Quickly he corrected that. "Well, if someone asks me about the accident in front of her, or if the subject comes up, I don't avoid talking about it. I just try to say as little as possible. I don't know how much she remembers or how painful it is for her to remember."

"Probably very painful," Tanya acknowledged. "So painful her mind is blocking her ability to talk about it. I don't know what the doctors told you to do, but I'd suggest you do talk to her about the accident, let her know that you understand how terrible it must have been and that you know she misses her mother. You can't pretend it didn't happen. What you can do is help her deal with it."

"At her age, though?" He wasn't sure.

"Don't underestimate a four-year-old. Also, when you feel she's ready, you should start leaving her for short periods of time." Tanya glanced at Sasha, then back at Ross. "Give me a call sometime, and I'll watch her when you two go out."

"We're not dating," Sasha said quickly.

Ross nodded. "I'll do that."

"We're not dating," Sasha repeated.

"I heard you." Tanya smiled—the same all-knowing smile she'd always smiled when they were growing up and she knew something Sasha didn't. "So are you going to let me taste some of that goat cheese you said you made?"

"We are *not* dating," Sasha mumbled under her breath as she headed for the refrigerator.

Ross stayed another hour. He also tasted some of the goat cheese and found it to his liking, though Jenny wrinkled up her nose when offered a piece and refused to even try it.

Before he left, they all went outside to look at the porch. Ross tested the boards and agreed with Sasha that they all needed to be replaced. He'd known that the first time he saw it. Then he walked around the house, thumping on the wooden exterior and crouching to check the stone foundation. From front to back and then around to the front again, he thoroughly inspected the building's structure. Finally he returned to where Tanya and Sasha stood. "You're going to have to replace a few boards here and there and patch up some mortar, but with the exception of the porch the house is quite solid. Probably last another hundred years. How's the roof? Any leaks?"

Sasha grinned. "Only when it rains. How's a lawyer know so much about house construction?"

"It's my father's business. He's headed Hammond Construction ever since I can remember. And I spent a lot of summers working for him. I think for a while he thought I might want to take over. After you tear this porch off, are you going to put another one up?"

She stared at the rotten boards. "Until I get some money, I'm not putting anything up—porch, wallpaper or windows."

Ross said nothing, but his mind was working.

MONDAY AFTERNOON he drove into her yard again. Sasha had been at her sewing machine since early morning, making the clothes that would be worn by the dolls she'd completed the week before. Quality was the mark of her creations. She used only the best materials, and most of the stitching was done by hand, every detail carefully worked in to give each doll a uniqueness its owner would appreciate.

Each of the My Friends dolls had the two dimples on its bottom, a cute little navel, and overstitched button eyes that looked almost human; but otherwise no two were exactly alike. Even their colorful dresses, chemises, petticoats and lace-trimmed underpants differed. Many of the outfits did match ones Sasha made for herself; when buying material, it was easy to purchase extra.

Although Sasha used a sewing machine to stitch the seams on the clothes, she always did the finishing work by hand. She was working on an elegant blue taffeta dress when the dogs alerted her to Ross's arrival. She stepped outside just as Jenny scrambled out of the car. From her patio Sasha called a greeting to them.

"Hi. Beautiful day, isn't it?" Ross returned, absently patting Nero on the head as the black dog sniffed at the pant legs of his jeans.

It was a beautiful day—spring at its best. Flowering crocuses and daffodils edged the flagstone patio, and the fruit trees in the yard had started to bloom. The sky was a vibrant blue, not a cloud to be seen, and just a slight breeze moaned through the tops of the pines and pushed the skirt of Sasha's dress against her legs.

The nanny goat, grazing near a black oak, lifted her head to bleat at them, then trotted in their direction, only to stop when she came to the high fence that limited her freedom. Woefully the nanny bleated again.

Ross glanced in the goat's direction.

"She can't understand why she can't be in the yard like the dogs. Of course I'd hate to see what she'd do to my fruit trees if she was."

Ross looked different to Sasha today. More relaxed. It was his clothes, she decided. Since the day she'd run into him in the grocery store, she hadn't once seen him in jeans. The pair he was wearing now were definitely newer and cleaner than the others, but they looked comfortable. His pale blue sweater looked equally comfortable, the soft knit molding itself over his wide shoulders, and the color accentuating the blue of his eyes. He was also wearing Loafers—without socks.

Ross Hammond, you're starting to look like an average Putnam resident. She grinned at that thought. Ross would never look average, no matter what he wore...or didn't wear.

Jenny was also dressed in jeans and a sweater, and wore red-and-white tennis shoes. Her scarred cheeks were much more tanned than the first time Sasha had seen her. Nero and Polo sniffed at the little girl, and she pulled Anna away from their noses but didn't hesitate to pat each dog on the head.

"What brings you to Never-Neverland?" Sasha asked as Ross headed toward her.

"I have a business proposition to make."

"A business proposition?" Her eyebrows rose.

"Actually I have a question first." He stopped directly in front of her and looked around—taking in a shutter with a broken hinge, the paint peeling on the patio trellis and the boarded-up windows—then he let his gaze meet hers. "Have you asked for a loan at the bank? A personal loan so you can fix up this place?"

She laughed at the idea. "Let me tell you what the Putnam bank manager thinks about a woman who makes dolls and puts on puppet shows for a living. According to him, I'm not a good risk. In fact, he almost laughed when I asked him for a loan to buy this house. And so did three other bank managers I contacted. If Mr. Burk hadn't finally agreed to sell me this place under a personal agreement, I wouldn't be living here. No, I didn't ask for a loan to fix up this place. Why?"

"How would you like one?"

Sasha cocked her head. "The bank wants to give me a loan?"

"No. I do."

"You?" That really surprised her, and she straightened, her brows coming together. "I thought you considered this place a bad buy."

"I consider it unsafe. At least the porch was." Coming down her drive, he'd noticed she'd completely torn the porch off, and the rotten boards were now in a neat pile some distance from the house. "This place needs a lot of work, but I think what you've done so far is great. By the time you're finished, you'll probably have doubled its value."

"Ross, I'm not fixing this place up to make money. I don't want to sell it."

"I understand that."

She frowned. "Do you realize that some months I can barely make my house payments, take care of my utilities and buy food? Actually the bankers were right. I am a big risk. I never know how my dolls are going to sell."

"If you sign that contract, you'll have the money. If you don't sign, you can repay me in small amounts, skip payments if necessary. I don't need the cash right now, or I wouldn't be offering it to you."

"Ross, why *are* you offering it to me?"

"Because you need it."

"Sure." She laughed at the idea. "Come on, how naive do you think I am? Men don't offer women large amounts of money just because it's needed."

"This will be strictly a business deal," he assured her. "I'll expect you to pay the money back with interest."

"What kind of interest?" That was what worried her.

"Two points less than what the banks are asking now." He'd figured it out. He would come out ahead, and it wouldn't put too much of a financial burden on her. "Maybe I should ask how much money you need."

"You're serious?"

"I'm serious. How much do you need?"

"I'm not really sure," she confessed. She'd never sat down and figured out how much it would take to do all the repairs. Considering her lack of cash, that would have been too depressing. Since moving in she'd simply been tackling one job at a time, as she had the money.

"There is a catch."

"Oh?" Sasha felt a wave of disappointment. She'd figured as much.

"Or maybe I should say a request." He shifted his weight on his feet, not quite sure how to ask. In contract disputes he was considered decisive and unrelenting. Around Sasha he felt as awkward as a teenager, unsure of himself and afraid to speak up. "I, ah, I'd like to feel free to bring Jenny out here a couple of times a week."

Sasha looked at the child. Jenny was a few feet away, playing with the dogs. She'd put Anna astride Nero's back and was trying to get the Lab to move. Polo bounced around Jenny's legs, eager to please; Nero sat down.

"Here she seems to open up more. She's much more independent, she—"

Sasha glanced back at Ross. "You don't have to give me money to bring Jenny here."

"But if you had the money, you could go ahead with the repairs you want to make and I . . ." *I'd have an excuse to see you,* he wanted to say but knew he had to be more subtle. "I'm a pretty good handyman. Those summers working for my father taught me a lot. Though I've been known to hit my thumb a few times, I can swing a mean hammer. I could work on your roof, fix your windows."

She could use help with the windows. She'd discovered that when she repaired the ones in the kitchen. And she didn't relish climbing about on the roof. But if she said yes, she'd be seeing Ross on a regular basis, and that concerned her.

Seeing him just once a week at her story hour, she found it difficult to keep her eyes and thoughts off him. She didn't want to get involved; she kept telling herself that. She didn't want to think of Ross Hammond in romantic terms. *Damn!* If only the man weren't so intriguing ... so good-looking ... so ...

She looked into his eyes and tried to think of an excuse why it wouldn't work. "What about your law practice? Don't you need to get established? Shouldn't you be at your office, not here fixing my roof and windows? Why don't you just bring Jenny out and leave her with me a couple of times a week? I wouldn't mind."

"I don't think she's ready to be left. Not yet. And right now Jenny's welfare is more important than my law practice. I've put an ad in *The Mountain Messenger* listing my hours as by appointment only. Please, Sasha."

She couldn't refuse his plea. And maybe it would be for the best. Working with her, he'd see how different she was from most women, that her dolls and puppets weren't simply a pastime but a part of her. And maybe by getting to know him better she'd find flaws in his personality and get over this unusual attraction. Sasha nodded. "Your money and offer to help are accepted."

"Good."

THEY SPENT THAT afternoon going through her house, making a list of what needed to be done and what materials would have to be bought. Jenny tagged along, silently investigating every nook and corner of each room, tugging on Sasha's long skirt when she wanted her to show her something. A box of fabric scraps, too small even for doll bonnets but set aside for a quilt, became a treasure for the child. It was carried into the living room to be thoroughly investigated, while Ross sat at Sasha's kitchen table and made a detailed list of the lumber, hardware, stains, paints and other supplies needed. And as Jenny played and Ross jotted down estimates, Sasha fixed a meat loaf for three.

Jenny's eyes were growing heavy by the time dinner was eaten. The meat loaf dish was empty and a complete list of the necessary repair items was in his back pocket when Ross lifted his nodding daughter from her chair, grabbed her doll and prepared to leave.

Sasha walked with them to his car. By the time he'd finished buckling Jenny's seat belt, the child was almost asleep. "It's been a long day for her," he said, closing the car door as quietly as possible. "But she's getting stronger all the time. When she left the hospital, she had to have a nap every afternoon. Now she's skipping them on a regular basis."

"She looks better every time I see her."

"She does, doesn't she." Leaning back against the BMW's fender, he reached out and caught Sasha around her waist. Quickly he pulled her to him. "You also look better every time I see you."

"Ross!" she gasped, surprised to find her body so firmly nestled against his.

"Yes?" he murmured. Then his mouth covered her, silencing any possible protest.

And as his lips moved over hers, Sasha decided she didn't really want to object. His kisses felt too good. *He* felt good, smelled good—masculine. Her hands traveled slowly up over the soft fibers of his sweater to the solid strength of his shoulders. They'd shared an afternoon of friendship, and it seemed right that they should now share a few kisses of friendship. At least, that was the rationale she used to explain her lack of resistance.

But Ross's kisses quickly moved beyond the level of friendship. His tongue dipped into her mouth, sought hers and found it. And even knowing she should pull back, should stop before things went too far, she responded. Seductively her tongue parried with his.

He groaned and tightened his hold around her waist, wanting to absorb her totally. He'd held his desires in check all day, had decided it would be best to keep their relationship limited to a friendship, for now. But he hadn't been able to resist one kiss. One kiss had turned into many, and he thirsted for her. She felt soft yet firm, warm and alive and very exciting. He ached to know the feel of her skin against his, to hear her murmur words of love in his ear. No woman had ever felt so perfect to him.

Against her pelvic bone Sasha was aware of the hardening of his body and was certain he could tell her breasts were swelling, her nipples growing rigid. The evening sun had lost its heat and the mountain air was quite cool, but a fiery warmth licked over her. All reserve was abandoned, and she allowed herself to simply enjoy what was happening.

When she pulled back, her breathing was uneven. With eyes glazed she stared at his face. Shakily she tried to laugh off the need curling inside her. "You lawyers sure know how to catch a person off guard."

"I think it's more a matter of one certain person being too tempting to resist." So tempting he wanted to make love with her. A silly thought, considering he had a child asleep in the car. Knowing the impossibility of the situation, he dropped his hands from her waist.

Sasha stepped back, completely away from him, her legs wobbly, her mind dazed. "Ross...I...I thought we were going to be friends."

"We are friends. I don't kiss my enemies." He grinned at the idea, then pushed himself away from the fender. "Well, time for me to be going. Thanks for dinner. I'll transfer funds tomorrow and bring you a check."

"Ross..." Agreeing to take a loan from him had been a mistake. She knew that now. Being with him was too tempting. A fear she couldn't explain tore at her insides. "I've changed my mind. I can't take that loan."

"Sure you can. I thought we had this all settled. What's the problem?"

"I . . . That is . . ." For ten years she'd done what she wanted, when she wanted, how she wanted. She'd allowed no man to dominate her. Keeping control of her emotions had given her the leverage she needed. With Ross she seemed to lose that control. "It's a question of who's the boss."

"That's no problem. It's your house, you make the decisions. If it'll make you feel any better, I could write up a contract including the amount of the loan, payment methods, interest, and that you have complete control over how the money's spent. Would that satisfy you?"

Not entirely, but at least if it was in writing when he started telling her how to do things, she could bring up their agreement. And she was sure he'd tell her how to run her life. After eighteen years she'd grown to expect it from a man. "I guess so."

"Good. I'll bring it out tomorrow with the check."

Sasha remembered the doll dress she'd been working on earlier that day. It still needed to be finished. She could work late into the night but would also need time in the morning to finish all the details. "Come after lunch. Jenny can help me dress a new doll I've made."

ROSS AND JENNY came out the next day. He'd drawn up a contract. Sasha read it over carefully, gave her okay, then they both signed it. On Wednesday he brought Jenny to the story hour, and afterward he helped her load her boxes of dolls and puppets in her Chevy. Then the three of them walked over to the small restaurant in town and had lunch.

On Thursday he again showed up at her place. By Saturday "a couple of times a week" was turning into daily visits, and Nero and Polo were getting so that they welcomed the silver-and-black BMW with excited barking. They knew the car's arrival meant they'd have a playmate. Jenny would spend hours with the dogs.

Two weeks after Ross had contacted Benson Toys, the company sent a revised contract. Many of the clauses that Sasha had objected to had been deleted or altered, but not all the changes were to her satisfaction. Quality control was still the item that concerned her most, and on that the company had hedged, rewording the section but not really giving her any say. Ross advised her not to sign.

The next day he phoned Benson Toys, and a conference call was set up. Benjamin Bernstein, Sasha, Ross and the company's lawyer discussed the problem, and Bernstein assured them the matter could be resolved. Sasha hoped so. When she hung up the phone, she was glad Ross had been on the line to back her up.

To express her appreciation she held another tea party for Jenny, this time including Mandy and her mother. Ross worked on rehanging shutters while Sasha told the girls stories and Mandy's mother, Ruth, stood by and listened. Before long the two girls were playing with the dolls on their own, with Mandy more than content to do all of the talking and Jenny gesturing whenever she wanted something. Sasha and Ruth went inside to make a cup of tea for themselves.

Ross could see his daughter was happy. Jenny didn't even notice when he left to drive into Putnam to pick up some hinges. Nor did she seem particularly upset when he returned half an hour later. A smile and a wave was all she gave him, then she took off with Mandy to go see the goat. Soon, he knew, he could take Sasha's sister up on her offer to baby-sit.

THE NEXT TUESDAY, Sasha was scheduled to put on a puppet show at Indian Bear Elementary. The school was just off Highway 49 on the way to Truckee. She suggested that Jenny might enjoy watching the show, and Ross willingly offered to drive. He pulled into Sasha's yard early Tuesday morning, let Jenny out and opened the trunk. Then he went into the house to help Sasha load the puppets and stage set she'd said she'd be taking.

When Ross came back out, he was carrying a large box. Sasha was still inside, making sure all the parts of the stage set were together, and Jenny had been waylaid in the living room by the sight of a new doll. He was almost to his car when he heard Nero. The three-legged Lab was barking wildly, and so was Polo.

Stopping, Ross turned in the direction of the sound. He saw the dogs as they came around the corner of the house at a dead run. He also saw the striped tomcat they were chasing. The cat dashed straight between his legs. Ross stood where he was and hoped the dogs would swerve.

Polo did; Nero didn't.

By the time Sasha and Jenny came out of the house, Ross was back on his feet and had brushed off most of the dirt and gravel. The knees of his favorite tan slacks, however, were now snagged, and his mood was a little less jovial than when he'd first arrived.

His mood didn't improve when they tried to fit the dismantled puppet set into the BMW's trunk. No matter how they angled the pieces, one always wouldn't quite fit. Finally they left Sasha's yard with Jenny sitting in the front seat and Sasha in the back, scooted slightly forward. Behind her a brightly painted, lightweight plywood wall blocked the BMW's rearview mirror.

Ross had allowed what he thought was ample time to make the drive to Indian Bear Elementary but discovered he hadn't bargained on every slow-moving vehicle in the state of California being on the twisting, turning mountain road that day. They arrived at the school just fifteen minutes before her show was scheduled to start.

He was glad Sasha knew how all the parts of the puppet-show set fit together. After pinching a finger between two sections, Ross decided to simply bring her what she needed and let her do the work. By the time he left the stage, carrying Jenny, he was ready to sit down and relax.

But that was not to be. Every chair in the gym was filled by a student or teacher. The few parents who had come to watch stood back against the walls, which was where Ross headed. Holding Jenny in his arms so that she could see the stage easily, he leaned against a wall and waited for the show to begin.

Onstage a gray-haired woman scampered from the microphone to the sound box. "Testing . . . testing," she repeated, a hair-raising screech filling the air and going straight through Ross's head.

She finally got the sound level balanced and introduced Sasha. The children all yelled, applauded and stomped their feet. Ross could tell it wasn't going to be a quiet audience. He could also feel the start of a headache.

Sasha pulled Clancy the Clown out from behind the puppet set and, without using the microphone the woman had so dutifully set up, began the show. Her voice carried clearly to every corner of the gym, and peals of laughter greeted the marionette's tales of life at

Clown Elementary School. Traveling back and forth along the front of the stage, she involved every child in the gym in her tale.

"This is her third year to put on a show. She's crazy, but they love her."

At the sound of the deep, very masculine voice, Ross turned his head. A tall, dark-haired man with the build of a lumberjack had come up to stand next to him.

"I think *I* love her," the guy murmured suggestively, and Ross bristled.

There was a cockiness to the man's stance that dared rebuttal, a subtle flexing of muscles that issued a challenge and an arrogant boldness in the way he was looking at Sasha's breasts. Under his breath he said what was on his mind: "What I'd love is to get my hands on those."

Immediately—without thinking—Ross responded. "You touch one inch of that woman and you'll wonder what hit you."

The threat came out more loudly than he'd expected but might have gone unnoticed if Sasha hadn't held up a hand at that moment, asking for quiet. The result was that the only voice audible in the gym was Ross's. He might as well have used the microphone.

Sasha stared directly at him.

Jenny twisted in his arms to face him, and all the children, teachers and parents turned his way.

Giving a low, sardonic chuckle the man with the lumberjack build backed away from Ross and slipped out the nearest door.

Ross could feel his face growing uncomfortably hot. He didn't know what to say or do, and a definite throb tortured his head.

"Hey, is this Indian Bear School?" a high-pitched voice cried out from the stage. Eyes turned forward again to see a pink-haired hand puppet moving about in Sasha's set. "Where are the bears?"

"Bears! Bears! Oh, no! Where are the bears?" Another hand puppet popped up, ran into the pink-haired one, then backed up. The children laughed. Jenny clapped her hands in delight, and Ross sighed. Sasha had managed to divert everyone's attention.

At the moment he would have liked to slip out of the gym, but that idea presented two problems. One, his daughter was thoroughly enjoying herself and would undoubtedly put up a fuss—albeit a silent one—if he left. And two, if he left, he might run into the lumberjack, and considering the man's size and weight, Ross wasn't sure he wanted to have to back up his threat. Much as he loved a good verbal sparring, he'd never been into physical violence. He decided he couldn't possibly leave when Jenny was having so much fun.

6

SASHA WASN'T REALLY sure what to say to Ross after the puppet show. From the statement that had echoed through the gym, she had an idea of what had transpired between the two men. In the past three years every time she'd been at Indian Bear Elementary School, George Keller had harassed her. He hadn't bothered to disguise the lust in his eyes and just last fall had told her he wanted to go to bed with her. He'd been surprised when she refused.

His being the school's principal made the situation tacky. She'd been dreading this spring performance. So when Ross had offered to go along, she'd been delighted. She'd hoped his presence would create a buffer, that she could put on her show and leave without incident. It seemed that was not to be.

"I made a fool of myself today, didn't I?" Ross sighed as he drove the three of them back toward Putnam.

Sasha leaned forward, resting her arms along the back of Jenny's seat. Ross's threat had probably cost her financially. She doubted if the Doll Lady would be called to Indian Bear Elementary again. But she didn't care. "George Keller is a pain in the—" considering that Jenny was sitting in front of her, Sasha picked a suitable word "—neck. The school system must have been desperate to have picked him to be principal."

"He's the principal?" Ross groaned. His headache was now full-blown.

Sasha laughed and reached forward to touch the sleeve of his cable-knit sweater. "Hey, don't worry about it."

He glanced down at her hand, back at her face, then looked forward again. He had a feeling he'd really messed things up for her. "Me and my big mouth. It's just that when he said . . ." Ross didn't finish. He'd reacted like a jealous lover, and anything he might say now would only make matters worse.

Sasha didn't need to ask what George had said. She gave Ross's arm an understanding squeeze, then let go. "I appreciate your coming to my defense."

"Some defense," he grumbled, then chuckled. "The guy would have probably creamed me. You two want to stop somewhere for lunch?"

Jenny bobbed her head up and down and bounced on the seat. The child was full of energy. Ross, on the other hand, looked drained. Lines of tension edged his mouth, and his forehead was furrowed. "Whatever you want to do," Sasha said willingly.

"Stop for lunch." He hoped food and a couple of aspirins would ease the throbbing in his temples. He felt totally out of sorts.

They stopped at Bassett's Station near Gold Lake Road. He didn't feel much better when they left the restaurant. Although his stomach was full, his head still ached, and he was now irritated with Jenny for playing with her food. She'd ended up with peanut butter from her chin to her eyebrows. At least he'd been able to give her to Sasha to take to the women's rest room to wash up. Jenny might not talk, but every time he took her into a men's room, her eyes grew wide with curiosity, and he was sure he'd explained what a urinal was a hundred times by now.

It was after two when they arrived at Sasha's place. Jenny was still going strong and carried in Clancy the Clown, teasing the dogs with the puppet. "Be careful," Ross warned her. "Don't mess up the strings, or Sasha will be mad."

By the time they had finished bringing in the puppet set, Ross was ready to head home. He needed some time to unwind, a chance to think over his jealous reaction that morning and more aspirins for his headache. He was in no mood to walk into Sasha's living room and discover that Jenny had opened the tole-painted steamer truck and was busy pulling out every marionette Sasha owned. On the floor by the child's feet lay a tangle of wooden bodies and strings.

Eyes narrowed and body rigid, he bellowed her name. "Jennifer Marie Hammond, what are you doing? How many times have I told you not to—"

"Don't yell at her!" Sasha ordered sharply from behind.

Surprised by the fervor of her words, Ross turned to face her. "But she—"

"You are *never* to yell at a child while you are in my house! Never! Do you understand?"

"Sasha, this is my daughter. I'll disa—"

"Never!" she repeated firmly and walked over to kneel beside Jenny. She'd been yelled at often enough as a child to know how cutting and painful a father's words could be.

Confused and irritated by Sasha's response, Ross stared at the tangle of marionettes on the floor. "Look what she's done. Don't you care?"

"What she's done is pulled out some toys. That's all!"

Jenny's wide blue eyes glistened with tears. One slid down her cheek over a scar, and Sasha wrapped her arms around the child. Ross said nothing.

For a moment Sasha simply held Jenny close, feeling the fragile warmth of her body. Then she gave her a final hug and kissed her damp cheek. Brushing a curly brown lock back from Jenny's face, she smiled at the child, and Jenny smiled back. Then Sasha turned her so that she faced the pile of marionettes. "You have made a mess, you know." Her voice was low and soothing. "What shall we do about it?"

Jenny stared at the puppets, then—eyes still glistening with tears—knelt and picked up the top marionette. Its strings were already tangled with the strings of the next one down, and that marionette also moved. Jenny stopped and tried to unravel the strings. They came apart and she looked at Sasha, smiled proudly and handed her the freed puppet.

Sasha took it and placed it back in the trunk. "That's good. Now go on. There are more."

The next marionette on the pile was more thoroughly tangled. For a while Jenny worked on it, then stopped, and with tears of frustration filling her eyes, again looked at Sasha.

"Not so easy, is it? I keep them in this trunk so they won't get tangled up. In the trunk they each have a spot. If you wanted one, you should have asked."

Jenny pointed to her mouth and shook her head.

Sasha also shook her head. "That's no excuse. You could have let me know what you wanted. Now, you must help me straighten these out."

Ross watched as his daughter and Sasha worked with the puppets. It was obvious that her method of handling the situation was working, but he was too irritated to care. With a snort he turned and headed for the door.

It slammed behind him as he stepped outside. There'd been no reason for Sasha to jump all over him. Jenny was his child. It was his place to correct her. And it wasn't as though he'd been going to hit her. He'd never do that.

He paced in front of his car, eyes focused on the gravel drive, hands shoved into his pants pockets. All right, maybe there had been no reason for him to yell at his daughter—other than that he was tired, frustrated and his head still ached. No. No excuses. He was thirty-three; Jenny had just turned four. She might not be responsible for her actions, but he should be.

He stopped pacing, went to his car and slid behind the wheel. At the moment he didn't like himself all that well. He'd always thought being a good lawyer was a tough job. Being a good father, he was discovering, was even tougher. And understanding Sasha Peters was the most difficult task of all. What made that woman tick? And why was he so damn attracted to her?

When Jenny came out of the house, he was still sitting in his car, his head pressed against the steering wheel. His temples ached. The sound of Sasha's side door slamming brought his head up. With Anna in her arms, Jenny headed toward the BMW, then stopped and looked back. Sasha came out behind her.

Ross got out of the car, and Jenny skipped toward him.

"Did you get the puppets all put away?" he asked as she neared.

Her smile disappeared, she stopped skipping and her nod was barely discernible.

He could tell she was afraid he was going to scold her again. Instead, he walked toward her, lifted her into his arms and gave her a hug.

Jenny's wet mouth against his cheek told him she'd forgiven him, and his attention turned to Sasha. Was she still upset with him?

She came up to them, her eyes meeting his. "Thank you for all your help today."

"Some help. My interference probably cost you a job."

"There'll be other jobs. I'm glad you told him off."

"Nevertheless, I'm sorry." He glanced at Jenny, then back at Sasha. "For everything."

"Apology accepted—" she smiled "—for everything."

He hoped she meant it. "I think I'd better head home." Before he said anything else he'd regret. He'd been doing that too often today. "See you tomorrow."

"Tomorrow," she repeated.

Sasha watched the BMW pull out of her yard. He'd apologized; she hadn't. Maybe she should have. She wasn't sure. She knew she'd overreacted to Ross's raised voice; yet she felt a certain degree of justification. She'd named her home Never-Neverland, and like Sir James Barrie's island in *Peter Pan*, she wanted it to be a place where things would be as she wanted them—a place where she could be Wendy, telling stories to children; a place where no father would yell at his child; a happy home.

With a sigh she turned back to her house. She should have apologized. She'd do it tomorrow.

AFTER STORY HOUR the next morning, Mandy's mother came up to talk to her. Ruth was having problems with Mandy, and Sasha had noticed that the little girl was moody all morning, ready to fight anyone who opposed her view. By the time Ruth left, everyone was gone—including Ross and Jenny—and Emma was waiting to lock up. Sasha knew her apology would have to wait until Ross and Jenny came out to her place.

Only Ross didn't come out and work on her house that afternoon, and after three weeks of seeing him on almost a daily basis Sasha was surprised. By evening she was beginning to worry. Afraid something might have happened to him, she called his house. When he didn't answer, she decided to drive by his place.

His car was gone.

And it wasn't in the drive the next afternoon when Sasha looped by on her way to the post office. So, as casually as she could manage, she asked Wally Jones, the postmaster, if Ross had been in to pick up his mail. And Wally said that Ross had asked to have his mail held, that he'd be out of town for a few days.

That night, lying in bed staring at the ceiling, Sasha wondered why Ross hadn't told her he was going away...or when he'd decided to go. She had a feeling his departure and silence were related to the incident with the marionettes.

He yelled at Jenny, and I yelled at him, and he didn't like it. Now he'll show me. He'll leave me alone to think about what I've done. She'd certainly been sent to her room to "think things over" often enough as a child. She'd hated it.

Now that I know what he's like, she told herself, *I could never be interested in him.*

But she *was* interested in Ross Hammond, and all day Friday and Saturday she found herself on edge, listening for the crunch of car tires on gravel, waiting for the dogs to bark...hoping she'd be fixing dinner for three instead of one.

Saturday night she sat at her butcher-block table alone, absently pushing creamed tuna fish from one spot on her plate to another without taking a bite. She stared out her kitchen window but saw nothing. Her thoughts were on a blue-eyed man and his four-year-old daughter. She hated to admit it, but she missed the father more than the child.

On Sunday morning heavy gray clouds blocked out the sun. The wind whistled through the pines and the air was cold, crisply proclaiming that the calendar might say it was May but winter hadn't completely let go its hold. Sasha put on the green wool dress she'd worn to Ross's house less than a month before and drove into Putnam for church.

She was seated midway back from the pulpit, next to her sister and brother-in-law, Bruce. As she was waiting for the service to begin she saw Ross, dressed in a three-piece dark blue pin-striped suit. His attention was on Jenny as they walked down the aisle. He chose a pew slightly forward and on the opposite side of the aisle, and Sasha wasn't sure if he simply hadn't seen her or if he'd purposely kept his distance. She did know she was glad to see him again.

Children and adults stayed together for the opening hymns, prayers and a children's sermon, then the older children left for Sunday school, and weekly volunteers took the preschoolers to a room where they could play. Tanya was one of the volunteers this morning. With a smile she left her husband and Sasha and began to gather up the youngsters closest to her. She had a two-year-old boy in her arms when she stopped at Ross's pew. Quietly she asked if Jenny wanted to go.

Sasha watched as Ross whispered to his daughter. Jenny shook her head. Tanya said something, but Jenny shook her head again. Then Ross leaned close, his expression stern as he spoke to his daughter. Jenny nodded slowly—blue eyes brimming with tears—and slid off the wooden bench. Her mouth in a tight line, she took

Tanya's free hand and walked silently, rigidly, down the aisle. Sasha saw a tear trickle down the little girl's cheek.

Ross watched until Jenny disappeared through the doorway at the back. He was turning to face forward again when he saw her. His smile came quickly, a warm welcome that embraced her, and Sasha knew then that he hadn't realized she was there. Then his gaze moved to her side, to rest on her brother-in-law's face. Ross's smile died on his lips, and he quickly turned toward the front of the church. It was then that the minister began his sermon.

As soon as the benediction was given and the congregation began to leave, Bruce headed out of the sanctuary to help Tanya. Sasha was in the aisle, moving slowly toward the spot where the minister was greeting people, when Ross edged up next to her. "Good morning, Miss Peters."

She turned toward him. His voice had been cool. Hers was cheerful. "Good morning, Mr. Hammond."

For a moment his gaze caressed her face, then he looked around the room. "You seem to have lost your escort."

"Bruce went to help Tanya clean up."

"To help Tanya?"

She nodded. "You can tell they're still newlyweds. Most husbands avoid the nursery room like the plague."

Ross's smile was immediate. She'd been sitting next to her brother-in-law—not a suitor but a relative. He wanted to shout out his relief. He'd admit it; he'd been jealous. Jealous and hurt that in four short days she'd found someone else. Ever since he'd returned from Sacramento, late the night before, he'd been looking forward to seeing her again, had hoped she'd be at church. He'd wanted to apologize for his behavior Tuesday. Now he wondered how Sasha felt about his actions today. "I suppose you think I'm a terrible father for forcing Jenny to go with your sister this morning."

"I don't think you're a terrible father." If she could, she'd explain why his yelling at Jenny had upset her. But she couldn't. The reason was too personal.

"Your sister said she'd bring Jenny back if she was really miserable."

"Tanya would."

"They—the doctors—said I should get Jenny to do more on her own, that it would be good for her." Growing more and more uneasy about his decision, he glanced toward the minister. The line to greet the man was moving incredibly slowly, and most of the other children had rejoined their parents. But neither Tanya nor Jenny were to be seen.

Sasha could see he was concerned. "Come on. Reverend Cox won't remember if he spoke to us or not. Let's go check on Jenny."

The moment they stepped into the preschoolers' room, Ross's worries vanished. It was clear that Jenny was fine. Bruce was folding chairs and stacking them in a corner, and Jenny and another little girl were busy helping Tanya pick up toys. When Jenny saw her father, she smiled but didn't run to him. She simply continued picking up the toys and putting them back in the box at the front of the room. Only when the last toy was retrieved did Jenny find where she'd put Anna and then head his way. Her earlier tears had been replaced by a broad smile. He gathered her into his arms and gave her a hug. "Did you have a good time?"

Jenny nodded vigorously.

The other little girl ran past them to go to her mother. Jenny snuggled against her father, then looked at Sasha and begged to go into her arms. Willingly Sasha took her. "So, how did you and my sister get along?" she asked, certain she already knew the answer.

Jenny checked where Tanya was. Her grin indicated they'd gotten along just fine.

Ross's eyes rested on Sasha and Jenny. It was good to see them together again.

"Ross, I'd like you to meet my brother-in-law, Bruce McDermott," Sasha said.

He shook hands with the good-looking rangy blond who had come up next to her, and was glad the man didn't know the jealous thoughts he'd harbored against him during the service that morning. Seeing the way Bruce watched Tanya, Ross knew he had no reason to be jealous.

"Bruce works for the forestry service. He and Tanya are coming over for lunch. Would you and Jenny like to join us?"

Jenny's head bobbed up and down.

Ross's answer was almost as eager. "Dinner sounds great."

SASHA HAD FIXED a stew, and Tanya brought a cake. After dropping by his place so that he and Jenny could change their clothes, Ross stopped at the store and picked up a gallon of ice cream. Later he discovered that rocky road didn't really go with pineapple upside-down cake.

It started to snow while they ate—a light snow that they knew wouldn't stay on the ground long. Nevertheless, the scene outside Sasha's kitchen window looked like a Christmas card, and after dinner Bruce and Ross brought in some wood and started a fire.

With Jenny's help Tanya and Sasha did the dishes, then they all sat around the fireplace drinking tea, instant

Look what we've got for you:

5 FREE GIFTS

... A FREE digital clock/calendar
... plus a sampler set of 4 terrific Harlequin Temptation® novels, specially selected by our editors.

FREE MYSTERY GIFT

... PLUS a surprise mystery gift that will delight you.

All this just for trying our Reader Service!

If you wish to continue in the Harlequin Reader Service®, you'll get 4 new Harlequin Temptation® novels every month—before they're available in stores. That's SNEAK PREVIEWS with 10% off the cover price on any books you keep (just $2.24★ each)—and FREE home delivery besides!

★Terms and prices subject to change without notice.

Get 4 FREE full-length Harlequin Temptation® novels.

Plus this lovely lucite clock/calendar

Plus a surprise free gift

▼ PLUS LOTS MORE! MAIL THIS CARD TODAY ▼

Harlequin's Best-Ever "Get Acquainted" Offer

Yes, I'll try the Harlequin Reader Service® under the terms outlined on the opposite page. Send me 4 free Harlequin Temptation® novels, a free digital clock/calendar and a free mystery gift.

142 CIH MDUJ

PLACE STICKER FOR 6 FREE GIFTS HERE.

NAME _____

ADDRESS _____ APT. ____

CITY _____

STATE _____ ZIP CODE ____

PRINTED IN U.S.A.

Don't forget...

. . . Return this card today and receive 4 free books, free digital clock/calendar and free mystery gift.

. . . You will receive books before they're available in stores and at a discount off the cover prices.

. . . No obligation to buy. You can cancel at any time by writing "cancel" on your statement or returning a shipment to us at our cost.

If offer card is missing, write to: Harlequin Reader Service,
901 Fuhrmann Blvd., P.O. Box 1867, Buffalo, N.Y. 14269-1867

coffee and orange juice. Talk flowed easily. Bruce was worried that the fire danger would be high that summer; Tanya was looking forward to school ending and having a chance to relax.

Ross told what had happened at Indian Bear Elementary School, with Sasha adding her point of view, and they all laughed, especially Tanya, who had met George Keller, knew his muscular build and could understand the humor in Ross's decision to stay and watch the end of Sasha's performance "for Jenny's sake."

For a long time Jenny sat with them, a silent listener, then—Anna tucked under her arm—she wandered over to play with the dolls by the trunk. None of the adults noticed when she left the living room.

After four o'clock Tanya and Bruce said goodbye. It had stopped snowing but was cold outside, and as soon as Bruce got the white truck started, Sasha closed the door. She turned to find Ross coming out of the kitchen. "I can't find Jenny," he said, in a voice edged with panic.

The child wasn't in the kitchen or the living room. Ross checked the bathroom, and Sasha went to her bedroom. At the doorway she paused. A whispered call and a wave of her hand brought Ross to her side. "We must have bored her with our talk."

With one arm looped over Anna, Jenny was asleep on the bed.

"Mind if I let her sleep a little while?" Ross asked quietly. He wanted to talk to Sasha.

"No problem." Sasha unfolded the afghan that lay at the foot of her bed and covered the child. Soundlessly Jenny snuggled under its warmth.

Together, Ross and Sasha returned to the living room. He went over and, using a poker, repositioned the half-burned logs in her fireplace, then added another. After closing the screen, he straightened and faced her. "Sasha, about what happened last Tuesday. . ."

She'd been restacking the craft magazines she and Tanya had looked through earlier. At Ross's words Sasha turned his way, ready with the apology she'd been prepared to give Wednesday. Then she hesitated. Had he left her alone for the past few days so she could "think" about the matter?

He wasn't exactly sure how to present his case. "I know it's just an excuse, but a lot of things had gone wrong that morning. I had a splitting headache, the. . ." He shrugged. "As I said, they're just excuses. And what I want to say is you were right. I shouldn't have yelled at Jenny."

It certainly didn't sound as if Ross had been waiting for her to acquiesce. "I could give some excuses, too, but I shouldn't have yelled at you, either."

He shook his head. "No, you were standing up for Jenny. I realize that and appreciate it. Also, as long as I'm apologizing, I should have let you know I was going away this week. I could have called you . . . but I didn't."

"Ross, you don't have to tell me where you go." No way was she going to admit she'd been upset because he hadn't told her.

"We're friends, aren't we?" He started from the fireplace toward her.

"Yes." Sasha focused her eyes on his face as he came nearer. His features were much more relaxed than they'd been Tuesday; his mouth now turned up in a slight smile. They were friends, but his warm blue gaze spoke of feelings far deeper than friendship.

Ross stopped directly in front of her. "Friends do tell each other what they're doing . . . where they're going." He touched her chin with a fingertip. "It was simply a spur-of-the-moment decision. I knew I had to take Jenny down to Sacramento on Friday to see the doctors, and I decided to go earlier so my folks and sister could see how Jenny's improved." Reverently he brushed his fingertips over the contour of her cheek and felt the softness of her skin.

He'd needed some time away from Sasha to think, but all he'd thought about was her. With the pad of his thumb he stroked the line of her lips. "I should have called, should have told you."

His light touch made her lips tingle, and she smiled and licked them. "It's all right. Really it is."

"No, it isn't. That's the kind of selfish behavior I used to inflict on Donna. I don't want to be that way with you." Cupping her chin with his hands, he lowered his head toward hers. "With you I want to be a better person, a likable person."

"Tanya and Bruce like you," Sasha whispered.

"And I like Tanya and Bruce," he murmured, a breath above her mouth. Lightly his lips brushed over hers. "And I like you," he added before angling his mouth a different way. "And missed you."

And I missed you... and your kisses, she answered without words. She wrapped her arms around his back and rose on her toes to bring their bodies into closer contact.

With kiss after kiss they repeated the unspoken message of mutual desire—each kiss longer, more consuming, more addictive. Behind Ross the fire crackled and popped, but Sasha was only aware of the secure warmth she felt in his arms and the heat her own body was generating.

When his hand moved to her side to stroke the curve of her breast, she responded by turning slightly to allow him greater access. His fingertips circled one rigid nub that pressed against the woolen material of her dress, then his palm rubbed over the point, and she groaned, a flurry of sensations shooting out in every direction. She could feel his arousal against her hips, the hardness of his body straining against the confines of his jeans. His desire excited her, and her longing to make love with him grew stronger and stronger.

"Sasha... Oh, Sasha." Between ragged breaths, his words were almost a litany. "I want to touch you... feel your skin against mine... look at you—all of you."

"Then do it," she responded hoarsely, the same need in her wiping out all hesitancy.

Reaching behind her, he pulled the zipper of her dress down to the small of her back, then stepped slightly away. He said nothing but his eyes were eloquent, his hands gentle as he drew her dress down to her waist.

Giddy with anticipation, she also remained silent.

Visually he caressed the creamy white skin straining to escape from the limits of her bra. Then he touched, slowly running a fingertip down from her left shoulder, over the cotton of her bra to the point of her nipple. Circling the sensitive area, he smiled, and Sasha held her breath, a tingling spreading to every nerve-ending in her body.

The circles grew larger as all his fingers came into play. Gently he pushed with the palm of his hand, staring at the way her breast flattened slightly. "So soft," he said in awe. "So very soft."

Her heart was racing, and she felt light-headed. Reaching behind, she tried to unsnap her bra. Ross realized what she was doing and did it for her. The cotton sagged, the straps slipped off her arms and her breasts were free.

For a moment he did nothing, said nothing, just stared at her voluptuous curves. Then he looked into her eyes and smiled shyly. "You know, I've always considered myself a leg man. With you, every part of your body is beautiful."

Sasha didn't know about being beautiful. She did know he made her feel very special, and when he kissed her, her legs turned to rubber. Grasping his arms, she used him for balance.

He didn't want to move too fast, but it wasn't easy for him to keep his desire in check. It had been over eight months since he'd been with his wife—with any woman. He'd once thought he had a low sex drive. Now he knew that wasn't true. He'd just needed the right woman. And Sasha was the right woman for him.

He could tell he was arousing her. He touched her face, and her skin was hot. He slid his fingers down her throat and felt the wild pounding of her pulse. With his lips never leaving hers, his hands played over her breasts, learning their contours, enjoying their fullness and teasing the hard peaks of her nipples. Her soft moans told him what he was doing to her.

He drove the tip of his tongue past her lips and brought his hips against hers. What he was doing to her, she was doing to him. His need for release was painful. He wanted to take her down to the floor, lift up her long skirt and bury himself within her. The thought fanned a fire within, and he stopped kissing her.

That wasn't the way he wanted to make love to her, not quickly, on the floor like an animal satisfying a primitive lust. He wanted to carry her into the bedroom, slowly finish undressing her, touch and kiss her until she begged for him to enter her.

Under his breath he swore. There was a definite glitch
to his plans. In Sasha's bedroom, on the only bed she
possessed, Jenny lay asleep. Frustrated, Ross wrapped
his arms around Sasha and held her close, silently
damning the fates.

"Are you all right?" Sasha asked, worried by the erratic rhythm of his breathing.

"Jenny's asleep on your bed," he groaned.

She was certain she understood. Jenny could wake up
at any time, and here she was, half undressed.

With a ragged breath Ross pulled back, gazed down
at her full breasts, then smiling, leaned over and kissed
the smooth skin above each rosy areola. In his puberty
he'd fantasized about women built like Sasha. At that
time in his life every difference between girls and boys
had excited him. As he'd grown older, the size of a fe-
male's breasts had become inconsequential. Only how a
woman could help his career had mattered.

Well, he no longer cared about his career, and in front
of him was perfection. His lips slid over a nipple, and he
sucked it into his mouth.

"Ross?" She groaned out his name.

Straightening, he grinned. "Just saying goodbye." He
stooped, picked up her bra and handed it to her.

With his assistance she put it back on, then he helped
her zip up her dress. Wrapping his arms around her, his
fingers entwined just below her breasts, he pulled her
back against him and kissed the nape of her neck.
"Sasha, I think we need to talk."

She agreed.

They sat on the sofa, his pant leg touching her skirt,
her hand in his. Gently he squeezed her fingers. "We're
friends, right?"

"Right." She definitely considered him a friend.

"And we're physically attracted to each other. Do you agree?"

Sasha hesitated for a moment, then quietly answered. "I agree."

"And if Jenny wasn't on your bed, we'd be making love right now."

"Maybe."

"No maybes about it. We would be." Leaning her way, he kissed her, then sat back and grinned. "I think it's time for me to start leaving Jenny with a baby-sitter."

"I'm not sure that's a good idea." She was thinking more clearly now. "I mean, you can leave Jenny with a baby-sitter if you want, but a few minutes ago, that . . . that may have been a mistake."

"That was no mistake."

She wasn't sure. "Remember the first time you kissed me? You said then that until Jenny was better, all we could be is friends, that she needs you."

"She has me. I'm not going to desert her, ignore her, because I feel this way about you. And I'm not going to revert to the uncaring cad I was before. But in case you haven't noticed, Sasha, Jenny is better. When I took her to the doctor's Friday, he said Jenny's improved tremendously."

"She still doesn't talk."

That was true. "While we were there, the doctor sent us to see one of the hospital's psychiatrists, Dr. Ryan. She ran some tests on Jenny and feels Jenny may be using her lack of speech to keep me close. She feels it's time I do start leaving her alone, at least for short periods of time.

"So yesterday I left Jenny with my mother and played nine holes of golf with my father, and last night I left her with both Mom and Dad and took my sister out to dinner. Mom said Jenny was fine both times. That's why this morning in church, when your sister asked if Jenny wanted to go with her, I decided to push a little . . . make her go. And you saw how she was when I picked her up."

Jenny had looked perfectly happy when Ross collected her after church. It seemed that excuse wasn't going to work.

"This afternoon Tanya repeated her offer to baby-sit. Jenny would be fine with her. How's dinner tomorrow night sound?"

"Tanya takes a class Monday nights."

"Then Tuesday night."

"Ross, we hardly know each other."

"And I'm suggesting we get to know each other better." He grinned and squeezed her fingers. "Sasha, we don't have to jump into bed Tuesday night. All I'm suggesting is dinner."

She knew better. There was a magnetism between them. Against her better judgment it drew her to him. Given the opportunity, they would make love Tuesday night. Chewing on her lower lip, her lipstick worn off long ago, she stared at Ross's face. Her past battled with the present.

Forget yesterday, live for today and hope for tomorrow. She told everyone that was her motto. Well, maybe it was time she started living. Truly living. Sasha nodded. "Where?"

"There's a nice restaurant in Downieville. Sits right on Main Street. I ate there last time I went to the courthouse."

She liked visiting Downieville. It was an interesting town. "A woman who makes teddy bears lives there."

"Good." He leaned close and gave her a quick kiss. "Before we have dinner, we can buy one and give it to Jenny when we get back."

7

DOWNIEVILLE WASN'T many miles from Putnam, but the steep, twisting highway made the distance seem greater. Named for Major Downie, an organizer of one of the first gold-mining camps from which the town grew, it was first called The Forks—a logical name, since two branches of the Yuba River met there. Surrounded by the Tahoe National Forest, the town hadn't grown much, but floods in years past had taken away many of the original houses. Still, some of the atmosphere of the 1850s gold-rush era remained.

Sasha had been to Downieville several times: to visit the woman who made the teddy bears, to put on puppet shows on Memorial Day and to attend the town's old-fashioned Fourth of July celebration. She knew Ross would be spending a lot of time there; Downieville was the county seat.

With the storm from Sunday long gone and the snow—except on the highest peaks—melted, the temperature was again pleasantly warm. Ross found a parking place directly in front of The Forks Restaurant, and the hostess led them to a table by the window. The few people already seated and eating looked up, their expressions curious. Sasha could understand why. Ross and she made an unusual-looking couple.

Her scoop-necked, floor-length, blue-and-green flowered cotton dress was a design from an 1850 catalog, and she knew she looked as though she'd stepped out of the Victorian age. Ross, on the other hand—in gray slacks, a pale blue cotton shirt, striped tie and navy sports jacket—was a twentieth-century man and dressed far more formally than anyone else in the restaurant.

From their table Sasha could look down on the patio below and the Downie River. Near the bridge two men wearing wet suits were sluicing for gold in the snow-fed water, while farther upstream, completely ignoring the men, a pair of white geese swam in lazy circles. Drawing her gaze away from the geese, Sasha studied the menu and tried to decide what sounded good. Actually she doubted she could eat anything. She'd been nervous about this date ever since Sunday. Her relationship with Ross was taking a new direction. She knew that. They both knew it.

Sasha glanced over the top of her menu and across the table to find Ross watching her. The look in his eyes turned her insides upside down. "Why don't you order for me?" she suggested, not really caring what she ate.

He ordered fresh mountain trout for both of them. And wine. The waitress brought two glasses of Chablis, and Ross lifted his. "To us . . . and to tonight."

He took a sip, smiled and Sasha felt her stomach do another flip. *Tonight.* Was she ready? Without a word, her gaze never leaving his face, she sipped some of her wine, then put down the glass. "What about Jenny?"

Ross frowned. "What about Jenny?"

"You told Tanya you'd pick her up before nine."

He glanced at his watch. They'd left Putnam early so that they could stop and buy Jenny a teddy bear before dinner. It was barely six o'clock. "Unless service is very slow here, we should be done by then."

"They do advertise leisure dining, you know." Sasha laughed. Perhaps dinner was all he was talking about.

Perhaps she was the one pushing them into bed. "So how's the lawyer business doing? I heard you tell Tanya that you've been getting some clients."

"A few." He liked the sound of her laughter. "I made up a will last week, filed a deed and yesterday I talked to a woman who's considering divorcing her husband." Sasha raised her eyebrows, but he shook his head. "I can't tell you who, but considering Putnam's very efficient grapevine, I'm sure you'll know soon enough."

She imagined she would. Putnam's grapevine was indeed very efficient. Lately she'd been hearing her name linked with Ross's. Even Emma, the librarian, knew he'd gone with her to Indian Bear Elementary School, though she'd never mentioned it to her. "Any regrets that you left Sacramento?" she asked, curious.

"No." He took another sip of his wine. "Oh, sometimes I miss the challenges, but I think in time I'll build up a decent practice here. I was such a one-sided person before. A year ago, if I wasn't at work, I was thinking about it. I'd go to the office early, stay late, work weekends. Even when I went home, I took my work with me. If I played handball or golf, it was to make contacts. I didn't know how to relax and enjoy myself. I was a true workaholic."

"And after the accident you just quit being one?" From the way he'd just described himself, she had a feeling it hadn't been that easy.

"Jenny's condition more or less stopped me cold turkey. Those first few days after the accident were touch and go, and I didn't dare leave her for any length of time. I certainly couldn't work, not as upset as I was. And sitting by her bedside, I had a lot of time to think about my life and what I'd accomplished. The only thing that really seemed worthwhile was lying next to me, on the brink of death.

"By the time she started to respond and the doctors said she'd live, I knew I wanted to change my life. I talked to the psychiatrist at the hospital, then read everything I could about workaholics." He chuckled. "The way I went at it at first was in true workaholic fashion. Every spare moment was devoted to learning and thinking about my problem.

"Anyway, when I went back to work, I started putting what I'd learned into practice. I started setting realistic goals, limited the time I'd spend at the office, and wouldn't take any papers home with me. At first I did pretty well, then I started slipping back into old habits, and I knew the best thing for Jenny and me would be for me to pull out of the firm completely, move up here and make a fresh start. And you know the rest."

She knew he was still struggling with his habit—that sometimes when they were working on the house, she had to insist he stop or he would go on with a project until it was completely finished, no matter how long it took. And she knew it was still hard for him to relax. Completely relax. But he was trying. She also knew he was a conscientious worker and did a good job—be it on her house or in negotiating her contract. Sacramento's loss was Putnam's gain.

Over their dinners they talked about the work that still needed to be done on her house, wondered what Benson Toys's next move would be and tried to think of ways to encourage Jenny to talk. When Sasha realized she'd eaten all of her trout, she decided it was the wine that had whetted her appetite. The wine was also making her feel very mellow and relaxed. She was sure she could sit and listen to Ross talk forever.

It was just starting to get dark when they left the restaurant. As they headed back to Putnam, Sasha looked over the teddy bear Ross had bought for Jenny, closely checking its construction.

"Think she'll like it?" he asked.

"She'll love it." Sasha straightened the bow tie under the bear's neck. "Wish I'd thought of making something like this. Do you realize that if I sign that contract, I won't be able to make any more of the My Friends dolls? I'm going to have to come up with another idea."

"Do you realize how much money you're going to get for those Friend dolls?"

She smiled, then laughed. "Not much after I pay you."

"I'm not *that* expensive." He glanced her way. "Want to negotiate?"

His seductive grin told her what he'd be negotiating for, and once again her stomach flipped. "You're going to have to drop me off at my place, then pick up Jenny and go home. We won't have time to negotiate."

"We could pick up Jenny and go to my place," Ross suggested. He'd been hoping that that was how the evening would end.

"And then how would I get home?" She knew he wouldn't leave Jenny alone.

"You could spend the night." Again he glanced her way. It was up to her.

For a moment she stared at him, not quite sure what to say. His proposition was tempting; she'd admit that. It was also impossible. "Ross, you know how people talk in this town. I'm the Doll Lady. I work with little kids. I have an image to uphold. If someone saw me come out of your place tomorrow morning . . ." Shaking her head, she half laughed, half groaned. "It just wouldn't work."

"Your place, then? Not to spend the night, but for a while. We could put Jenny down and then . . ." He left it to her imagination.

"I have only the one bed." She'd never needed more. Her parents certainly wouldn't be coming to visit her.

He pulled over to the edge of the road and stopped the car. Turning in his seat, he faced her. "Sasha, I want to be with you."

"I know." Closing her eyes, she took in a deep breath. She needed to think clearly, but her mind seemed fogged.

"I want to make love with you."

"I know," she repeated, the words barely audible.

"Do you want to make love with me?"

Her flaxen lashes fluttered against her cheeks, then raised. She stared into his eyes.

"I don't know what I want." The freedom to be her own person; the warmth she felt whenever he was around. Independence. Companionship. Her needs were in conflict.

For a second he considered her answer, then once again faced forward and started the car. "We're going to pick up Jenny. Then we'll go to your place. Whether I stay or simply drop you off will be your decision."

"AS I SAID, she was a delight," Tanya repeated. "Once you were gone, the tears disappeared, and she helped me set the table and serve dinner. And after we did the dishes, I read a book to her. Then Bruce told her about the skunk that's decided to make her nursery under the rangers' headquarters."

Jenny snuggled against Ross, hugging his neck.

"We don't want to kill the skunk, but so far she's avoided all of our traps." Bruce chuckled, then reached out and patted Jenny's leg. "You've got a nice little girl here, Ross. If you ever decide you don't want her, we'll keep her."

"Oh, I'm keeping her," Ross said firmly. His daughter's bright smile when she'd looked up from Bruce's lap to see him, her running dash to his arms and her warm hug were precious gifts he'd never give away.

"But I hope you'll let her come see us once in a while," Tanya urged, stepping close to her husband. Tenderly she rubbed a hand over Jenny's back. "I told you he'd come back. Your daddy may leave you sometimes, but he'll come back."

"Thanks," Ross mouthed. Even though she couldn't say the words it was obvious Jenny had been afraid he wouldn't return. "See what I bought you?"

Jenny peeked out from the curve of his cheek, and Ross held the teddy bear up so she could see it. With a wide grin she leaned back and took the bear, studied it, squeezed it, then gave Ross a wet kiss on his cheek. From that point on, the bear stayed in Jenny's possession.

The grandfather clock in Tanya's living room was chiming nine o'clock when Ross slipped on Jenny's coat, gathered her back into his arms, along with Anna and the bear, thanked Tanya and Bruce and headed for the front door. Sasha kissed her sister's cheek, hugged her brother-in-law and followed Ross out to the car. Jenny was put in the back seat, and he drove to Sasha's. In front of her house he switched off the car's engine, unbuckled his seat belt and turned to face her. The dogs jumping up on the side of the car and barking were ignored.

"I enjoyed myself tonight," he said.

"I enjoyed myself, too." Her heart was beating as fast as a drumroll.

"I always enjoy being with you."

"Ross—" She stopped. She didn't know what to say.

"I'm not pushing you, Sasha. I'll never push you. The decision's yours."

Her palms were sweaty, her throat dry. Even her legs were shaking. She laughed self-consciously, then managed the important words. "Come on in."

He grinned and leaned forward to lightly kiss her lips. Then he straightened, opened his door and got out.

"DADDY AND SASHA want to talk for a little while," Ross explained to Jenny as he carried her into Sasha's bedroom. "So why don't you lie down here and go to sleep. You need to get a good night's sleep. Tomorrow's story hour, remember."

Obediently Jenny stretched out on the bed, with Anna on one side of her, the teddy bear on the other. It was already past her normal bedtime. Ross removed her shoes, and Sasha covered her with an afghan. Jenny kissed both of them, then closed her eyes. For a few minutes Ross and Sasha stood by the bed, watching the little girl, waiting until they were sure she was asleep. Then they tiptoed out of the room.

"Want some coffee?" Sasha asked, heading toward the kitchen.

Ross caught her wrist and stopped her forward progress. "No, I don't want any coffee."

"Tea?" she offered, her eyebrows rising as she turned back toward him.

"No." Slowly he drew her closer.

Sasha smiled. "Me?"

His satisfied grin made his sibilant "Yes" really unnecessary. She raised herself on her toes as he dipped his head. Midway their lips met.

Her nervousness disappeared. Whether it was right or wrong, there seemed no stopping the direction their relationship was taking.

"Oh, Sasha, what you do to me," he groaned against her mouth as he wrapped his arms tightly around her.

"This is probably a mistake."

"This is not a mistake." He kept kissing her, his hands moving over her back and through her hair. No, this wasn't a mistake.

His marriage to Donna had been a mistake. He'd married her for all the wrong reasons. He'd never wanted Donna as he did Sasha. No woman but Sasha had ever made him feel so content when she was near and so out of sorts when she was away. It was right with Sasha. He was sure of that.

His hands traveled to her sides, then around to the front of her dress. His fingers found the tiny buttons that held the bodice together, and one by one he began to release them. By the tenth he was getting frustrated. "Haven't you ever heard of Velcro?"

"They didn't have it in the nineteenth century." She laughed. She knew what a bear the buttons were. Every time she wore the dress, she cursed herself for not putting in a zipper. She could help him; instead, she reached over and began to unbutton his shirt.

"Just a minute." He left her buttons and stepped back, shrugged out of his jacket and tossed it onto her sofa. Next went his tie. In seconds he was back. "Now, where were we?"

Sasha laughed. "In the process of mutually undressing each other."

She tackled the next button on his shirt, and he continued with the ones on her dress. Having the easier task, Sasha finished first and pulled his shirt from his pants, then ran her hands over his bare chest. His skin was warm, his body lean and solid. Short honey-brown hairs curled against her palms. "Nice." She sighed.

He paused to look down at the slender fingers resting on his chest and smiled. "Very nice," he agreed, and leaned close to kiss her lips.

When the last of the buttons on her dress had been released, he slipped the material off her shoulders and down her arms, exposing the beige bra she'd worn underneath. Turning her, he undid the clasp and slipped it off. Then he brought her back around so that she faced him. Ever since Sunday he'd wanted to see Sasha like this again . . . to touch her.

Wrapping his arms around her, he drew her close so her breasts pressed against his bare chest. His shirt got in the way on one side, and he pulled it free, then changed his mind and took the shirt off completely, managing in the process to maintain contact between their bodies. The feel of her nipples against his skin, combined with months of abstinence, were almost more than he could bear, yet he loved it. Free of his shirt, he brought his hands back into play—touching, stroking and massaging every inch of soft velvety skin that he could reach.

She groaned when he leaned down and kissed a breast, then sucked the nipple into his mouth. Her legs felt weak, and she wanted to lie down. Pelvic muscles were tightening, and she could feel a moist warmth dampen her panties. It had been a long time since she'd made love. Her body ached for a union. Combing her fingers through Ross's thick hair, she stared blankly over his head. In a haze she saw the little girl standing in the bedroom doorway.

It took a second before the sight registered. Another before she responded.

"Ross," she rasped, her fingers tightening their hold on his head.

He continued to suck on her nipple, his fingers gently kneading her breast.

"Ross," she said more loudly and strongly and pushed his head back. "Jenny."

Hearing his daughter's name didn't explain a thing, but the urgency in Sasha's voice was enough to bring his eyes up. She was staring behind him. Following the direction of her gaze, he looked, saw and groaned. "Jenny."

The child didn't move from the doorway. Slowly Ross straightened to his full height, then went to his daughter. Turning her back to Jenny, Sasha slipped her arms into the dress's puffed sleeves and pulled the material up. She wasn't going to bother with her bra—not under the circumstances. Quickly she buttoned every fourth button, more or less. Enough to close the front.

By the time Sasha felt she was decently enough covered to face them again, Ross had picked Jenny up and was walking toward the kitchen. He gave her a rueful smile. "She's thirsty."

Sasha ran her tongue over kiss-swollen lips. "So am I."

"Well, it's not what I am," he grumbled, carrying Jenny to the counter. Seconds later the child had her drink.

Sasha came over to stand by them. From her cupboard she also got a glass. After she'd drunk some cold water, she felt better. Looking at Ross, she didn't know what to say. Frustration was painted all over his face. What had happened wasn't funny. She knew it wasn't. Still, she couldn't help herself. Remembering what they'd just been doing, her shock at seeing Jenny and Ross's groan, Sasha started laughing.

At first Ross glared at her, then a grin started at the corners of his mouth, grew wider and spread to his eyes. In moments he, too, was laughing.

"I said it would be a mistake," she said, trying to stop laughing.

"This arrangement certainly isn't working out," he agreed.

"Maybe we're just supposed to be friends."

"Forget that idea."

"So, what do you suggest?"

"I don't know." Holding Jenny in his arms, he leaned back against the counter and stared through the kitchen doorway into the living room. Beyond that room was the closed door of a bedroom that was in need of much repair. A slow smile played on his lips. "On the other hand, maybe I do know what to do. If we fix up that extra bedroom . . . buy a bed for it . . ."

Sasha could see his plan. "Jenny would have a room, and so would we."

"And she knows not to enter a bedroom if the door's closed."

WEDNESDAY AFTERNOON they started working on the bedroom. For the next few weeks, Ross tackled the job with the energy of a true workaholic. Old wallpaper was peeled from the walls, holes were patched, windows replaced, the ceiling was painted and the floor was stripped and revarnished. During that time the revised contract from Benson Toys arrived. Ross and Sasha took a break to read it through several times. "Looks good to me," he said. "I can't see any reason you shouldn't sign it."

So she did.

Two days after she'd mailed it back, she received a telephone call. Ross was trimming wallpaper when Sasha came into the room, smiling. "How long do you think you could be away from Jenny?"

He looked up from the strip of paper he was cutting, a slight frown furrowing his brow. "I don't know. Why? What's up?"

"That was Benjamin Bernstein. Now that I've signed the contract, they want to push production on the doll, have it out for Christmas. They already have a prototype made up that they want my approval on. And they want to do some publicity pictures with me signing the contract, looking at the doll in production. I don't know what all."

She stopped next to Ross. "They want me to come down to San Francisco Friday."

"And you want me along?"

"Well, as my lawyer, it would be nice. I mean, you never know when a legal question might come up." She grinned. "There's going to be a dinner in my honor that night. A late dinner. We'd have to stay over...in a hotel."

His grin matched hers. "Yes, I think you'd better have your lawyer along."

BRUCE SAID HE would milk the goat and feed the animals. Ross decided to leave Jenny with his folks in Sacramento. She was more familiar with them. The sun's early-morning rays were changing the slate-gray cliffs behind Sasha's house to gold when she climbed into the BMW. Jenny, in the back seat, responded with a sleepy nod. They stopped for breakfast in Grass Valley, and it was still quite early when they arrived at Ross's parents' home.

Although the neighborhood, the size of the Hammonds' house and yard, and the make of the cars in their driveway indicated wealth, Sasha found both of Ross's parents to be delightful, unaffected people. She envied Ross the acceptance she heard in his father's voice. And their words of congratulation to her were warm and sincere. That they adored their grandchild was obvious. And though Jenny pouted and tears slipped down her cheeks when Ross told her it was time for him to leave, Sasha had a feeling the little girl would be well entertained for the next thirty-six hours and wouldn't miss her father for long.

They arrived in San Francisco just a bit after ten o'clock, found Benson Toys, and pulled into a visitors' parking spot. While Ross came around to open her door, Sasha checked her makeup. Studying her reflection in the mirror, she poked at her hair with her fingers and frowned. Naturally curly hair had its drawbacks. It seemed to always do what it wanted, and today it had a wild, tangled appearance.

"You look beautiful," Ross said, patiently waiting for her.

"I look—" With a sigh and a shrug she put the mirror away and turned to get out. "I look like I look, and they'll have to take me that way." Grasping Ross's hand, she gave it a squeeze. "I'm glad you said you'd come along. I'm a nervous wreck."

"You don't look nervous." Leaning closer, he kissed her lips, then squeezed her fingers back. "Relax. Just remember, you have the right to reject what they're going to show you today. They're the ones working on ulcers right now."

"Does give one a feeling of power." She grinned. "Bernstein said they were going to pick up the bill for the hotel room. Think if I reject their design they'll still pay?"

"I don't know. But if not, I'll pay for it."

NEITHER BENSON TOYS nor Sasha needed to worry. She was delighted with the doll Benjamin Bernstein showed her. Although the workmanship wasn't of the same quality as that of her own, hand-sewn creations, the material for the bodies was durable, the seams wouldn't easily come unstitched and the hair and eyes looked realistic and wouldn't be hazardous to young children.

"We're going to call them Victorian Friends," he told them. "Each doll will have a title—Lady Susan, Lady Ann, Little Lord Robert.... And each will have an official-looking paper naming the estate he or she supposedly owns."

He showed Sasha and Ross drawings of the dolls they planned on manufacturing, each similar to but also different from one another.

"Of course they'll all have the navel and dimples," Bernstein went on, pointing out the features on the doll in her hands. "And they'll be dressed in Victorian clothes. In fact we're counting on the clothing to be one of the big money-makers with these dolls." He glanced over the pale green cotton Sasha was wearing. It had the modestly high neckline, sloping shoulders, floor-length bell-shaped skirt, full sleeves and small waistline of a typical Victorian day-dress. "I'm glad you came in costume."

She didn't bother to explain that she wasn't wearing a costume.

"I'll call our PR man in now," he continued. "He'll want to get some pictures that show you signing the contract, some of you looking over the doll and some of you checking out the assembly line. I hear you're called the Doll Lady. I think we'll use that in the press releases."

It turned out that John Mead, Benson Toys's public-relations man, wanted a lot of pictures. They set up a mock contract-signing and the cameraman prompted her to say "Money." And she did and smiled. Then she held the prototype of the doll in her hands, as though studying it, and smiled again as the camera clicked and the flash went off. Time and time again, she smiled until her cheeks began to ache.

Along the assembly line she pretended she was following the manufacturing process of the dolls from start to finish, but in reality it was an idle line, workers having been brought in just for the pictures. It would be a while before the Victorian Friends were ready for mass production.

During a luncheon put on by the company's board of directors, where Sasha was the honored guest, the camera continued to flash, and by midafternoon Sasha's cheeks were frozen into a perpetual grin, her eyes burned from the glare of the flash and she felt drained.

When at last they returned to Mr. Bernstein's office, she sank into a chair, exhausted. Near the window overlooking San Francisco's skyline, Ross, John Mead and Benjamin Bernstein stood talking about the economy, about the present attitude government had toward businesses and about the possibility of inflation. Sasha had no desire to break into the conversation.

She was content to watch Ross. From the moment they'd arrived at Benson Toys, he'd stayed in the background, but she'd been constantly aware of his presence. Even in silence he'd been supportive, there with a glass of water when she needed one, giving a comforting squeeze of her hand when she was feeling frazzled. He fit into this business world. She didn't, and was glad that this would be the extent of her contact with Benson Toys.

John Mead had suggested she might be an excellent spokesperson for the Victorian Friends—especially when Ross told him Sasha always wore nineteenth-century-style dresses. From lunchtime on, Mead had tried to talk her into signing a contract, promising that if she did she'd have appearances on *The Tonight Show*, *The Oprah Winfrey Show* and *Donahue*. She wasn't even tempted. Putnam was where she belonged, with her goat, cat, dogs, dolls and puppets. And with the children who came to hear her stories. She wondered, though, if Putnam was where Ross belonged, or if he was really just using the mountain town as an escape.

"Well. I imagine you'll want to rest up and change before dinner," Benjamin Bernstein said, turning away from the window and the other two men to face her. "We've reserved a room for you at the St. Francis Hotel. Dinner will be at eight. Cocktails at seven-thirty. Someone will pick you up around seven o'clock. All right with you?"

"Fine." They couldn't have chosen a nicer or probably more expensive hotel in San Francisco. And a few hours of rest did sound good.

Watching Ross come toward her, she smiled. Resting probably wasn't exactly what they would be doing.

8

FROM THE TWENTY-SIXTH floor of the St. Francis Hotel, Sasha could look down on Union Square. Shoppers scurried along the sidewalk, going from Neiman-Marcus to I. Magnin to Macy's and the other fashionable stores. Some stopped at the colorful flower stands, others flagged down cabs, waited for buses or headed underground for their parked cars.

In the two-and-a-half-acre park above the garage, young and old intermingled. Men and women in business suits hurried from one side to the other, a sense of determination in their strides. Tourists strolled, gawking at the sights and pausing to take pictures of the monument in the center or to admire a painting on display. Two old men played chess on an aged wooden bench, and a guitar player, sitting on the grass, was attracting a small crowd. Hundreds of pigeons—swirling about and strutting up and down—pestered them all.

Ross tipped the bellboy who'd brought up their two bags and closed the door behind him. Facing Sasha, he gazed at her back. The light coming through the window turned her hair into a silvery white halo, her body into a slim silhouette.

He knew the day at Benson Toys had been tiring for her. Her worries about the design of the doll and its production seemed to have been alleviated, but he'd noticed her smile was growing strained by the time

Bernstein and Mead had finished their picture-taking session. He should probably let her rest.

"Tired?" he asked, walking over to stand beside her. He, too, looked down at the bustling activity on the streets below. In the park a man and woman were strolling hand in hand. Ross slipped his arm around Sasha's shoulders.

She looked up at him. "I'm a little tired. What about you?"

"Not really." Leaning close, he kissed her on the temple, just below her hairline. She smelled sweet and womanly, and he wanted to absorb her.

"You enjoyed yourself today, didn't you?" She was sure he had, and that bothered her. For the first time she was afraid Ross might leave Putnam, that he'd change his mind and decide that the slow pace of life in a mountain town wasn't really what he wanted. "I think Bernstein would hire you in a minute. He seemed very impressed with you."

Ross chuckled and brushed his lips over her cheek, then nibbled his way to her ear. Maybe he'd gobble her up. "I'm not looking for a job. You know who impressed me? You. You handled all that picture-taking great."

"Maybe so, but I wouldn't want to make it a habit. Are you sure you don't miss it?" she asked, turning away from the window to face him. "Miss working with big companies? Working in the city?"

"Sure, I miss it," he confessed, letting his arms go around her. "Business law can be very exciting. Working with big-name executives and writing contracts that involve millions of dollars can be euphoric." He found her lips and kissed them.

It wasn't the answer Sasha had wanted to hear. Wrapping her arms around his back, she held him tightly. She was right; he would leave. And the idea of Ross no longer being in her life left her feeling empty. Her answering kiss had a sense of desperation to it.

"You make me euphoric," he groaned, hugging her even closer. "I should let you rest, but I don't want to."

"I don't need to rest." There would be time to rest when she was alone.

"So what would you like to do?"

Knowing this might be the only time they'd ever have together, her answer was easy. "I want to make love."

His grin was captivating. "Your wish is my command."

With a swoop he lifted her into his arms and carried her over to the bed. With one hand he pulled back the beige spread, the blanket and sheet. Placing her on the cotton bottom sheet, he sat beside her. "You know what I want?"

She'd thought it was the same thing she wanted. "What?"

"To see your legs. You don't know how frustrating it is for a leg man to fall—" He stopped himself and quickly changed what he was going to say. "To date a woman who wears long dresses."

"You want to see my legs?" Sasha laughed. Never before had she had a man ask her to bare her legs. Her chest, yes, but not her legs. "They're not that great to look at." Her father had certainly told her that often enough.

"Let me be the judge of that."

Sasha kicked off her high-heeled shoes and pulled the skirt of her dress up to show her ankles, her calves and most of her thighs. "So, what do you think."

"Sasha Peters." He shook his head and shifted his position so that he was sitting by her legs.

"That bad?"

"Bad?" His fingers moved smoothly over the nylon of her panty hose, and he chuckled. "Just the opposite. All this time I've been afraid you wore long dresses because you wanted to hide your legs." His hands slid over graceful contours. "But I was wrong. Your legs are beautiful."

"You really think so?"

"I know so." His fingertips moved sensually up over her calf muscles. "Why hide them?"

"I'm not." Or maybe she was. She wasn't sure.

"Why hide any part of you from me?" His hands traveled up to disappear under the folds of her skirt. Teasingly his fingertips neared unknown territory.

She ached for his touch and pulled her skirt even higher.

Immediately Ross experienced a tightening in his loins. "Oh, Sasha," he groaned and closed his eyes. "If only you knew what you do to me."

It was exhilarating to know she had power over him. Only it was a limited power. "I think maybe I do to you what you do to me."

His tawny lashes rose, and the blue of his eyes was darker than ever. Slowly he smiled. "I hope so."

He moved his fingertips higher to touch her between her legs, found the point of her pleasure and stroked her. Sasha sucked in a breath. There was electricity between them. She'd felt it the first day they met, and now it was traveling from his hand to every nerve-ending in her body. She leaned toward him and coiled her arms around his neck.

Ross kissed her, slipping his tongue into the moist cavern of her mouth. His fingers continued to excite her, teasing until she was writhing and unsure how long she could stand the sweet agony. One thing she knew—they both had too many clothes on.

As though reading her mind, he stopped what he was doing. Without saying a word, he got up and helped her to her feet. Standing behind her, he pulled the zipper of her dress down, then unclasped her bra. His hands came around to caress the fullness of her breasts, and he kissed the smooth skin of her shoulders and found the pulse point of her neck.

"So perfect," he murmured, his thumbs rubbing over hard, pointed nipples.

"So big," she corrected.

"Just right." He massaged each breast, enjoying the feel of her in his hands, then lifted her dress over her head, tossing it onto the nearest padded slipper-chair.

Next went her bra, then her petticoat, panty hose and panties. When she stood naked before him, he grinned. "I think maybe I like you wearing those long dresses. I don't want other men seeing this gorgeous body."

"Flattery will get you everywhere." Her fingers went to the buttons of his shirt, and it, along with his jacket and tie, was soon lying on the chair, over her things.

The buckle of his belt was easy, but she hesitated before pulling down the zipper of his slacks. Her eyes met his. He cupped her face in his hands and lightly kissed her lips. Looking into his eyes, she continued to undress him. Soon there was no hiding his desire, and she didn't pretend not to notice. He was every inch a man, proudly erect and blatantly masculine.

"I think I love you," Ross joked, looking down at himself.

A touch of nervousness curled inside her.

"Come here," he soothed and held out his arms.

She stepped closer, and the soft, tawny hairs on his chest touched her breasts and his erection pressed hot and hard against her stomach. His lips captured hers, and she forgot about being nervous. She swayed in his arms, and he groaned and stepped back, bringing her with him. At the bed he eased her down on the mattress, then stretched out beside her.

He knew he had to be careful, to go slowly. It had been so long since he'd been with a woman that his body was explosive, a time bomb just waiting to go off. If he wanted to treasure this moment, he had to stay in control.

His kisses were tender, his caresses light. From head to toe he made love to her, the tantalizing warmth of his lips and tongue following the stimulating strokes of his fingers. He loved the way she responded, the honesty of her actions.

Her readiness made it all the more difficult for him to hold back his need. Closing his eyes, he tried to concentrate on something besides the thought of being inside her. Then Sasha touched him. Lightly her fingers encircled his hard length. Gently she squeezed.

One stroke took him to the edge, and his eyes snapped open. "Don't—" he cried, but it was already too late. His release came in an instant.

"Damn." Embarrassed, he pressed his forehead against her shoulder. "Damn, damn, damn."

"Ross, it's all right," she murmured, quite aware of what had happened. Tenderly she kissed his forehead, then brushed her fingers through his hair. "It's all right."

"No, it isn't." He wrapped his arms around her and hugged her close. "I'm sorry. It's been so long...." He felt like a fool. An idiot. An immature teenager. "I wanted our first time to be perfect. I wanted to bring you pleasure, not—"

"You are bringing me pleasure," she insisted. Simply being with him, knowing him in this intimate manner gave her pleasure.

"You know what I mean."

"Yes. I know."

"I'm not usually like this. I don't usually... It's just been so long."

She kissed him and rubbed her hands over his back and shoulders and tried to tell him with her body that they had plenty of time.

Her breasts pressed against him, her nipples hard, and a tiny jolt of excitement stimulated nerves and muscles. Ross pulled back, surprised to discover his needs hadn't been completely sated. Smiling, he kissed her.

It took very little time before the desire to be inside her was once again motivating his every action. "Are you protected?" he asked.

Rubbing her palms over his shoulders, she nodded. The same week they'd started working on the bedroom for Jenny, she'd visited the doctor.

"Good." Otherwise, he would have seen to it that she was.

She arched forward and kissed the hollow of his throat. Huskily he ordered, "Look at me."

Letting herself sink back against the mattress, her long lashes barely rising, she looked up at his face. In her eyes he saw a yearning equal to his. "I love you," he whispered, then entered her.

The words meant nothing. She knew that and didn't care. At the moment all she wanted was for him to be a part of her, for him to fill her with his strength and bring relief to the ache he'd created.

Wrapping her arms around his shoulders, holding him close, she kissed him and arched her hips. His movements were slow as he searched for the spot that would give her the most pleasure. Each thrust took her closer, and she dug her fingers into his back and wrapped her legs around his hips. Breathing became an impossible feat, her skin was hot, and an internal fire flowed through her arteries.

And then it happened. Her body tensed, convulsed and the pulsating waves of pleasure began. Her mind soared to another realm. Ecstasy had meaning and paradise became a reality. Gripping Ross's arms, she cried out her joy.

And in time she relaxed.

"Oh, yes," Ross murmured, holding her close. "You feel so good."

"Yes, I do," she agreed, then realized he'd done everything for her. "But what about you?"

"I feel good, too."

"But—" She was sure he hadn't climaxed.

"Patience, my love." He kissed her cheek and chuckled. Be patient. That was what he was always telling himself.

He stilled his hips and waited until her breathing returned to normal. Then he again began to move.

Now he could let it come. Now he could allow himself to fully enjoy the perfection of her body, the exhilarating treasure of her femininity. His hips moved faster. His breathing became ragged, and the bed rocked with his motion.

When he cried out her name, Sasha had no doubt that he'd found the same satisfaction she had. With a sigh he collapsed on top of her.

FOR A MOMENT she thought Ross had passed out. His eyes were closed, his breathing was shallow and the weight of his body oppressive. Then his eyelids rose, and she could see the rich blue of his irises and the black of his pupils. He grinned and rolled off her onto his side.

"Now, that was nice," he confided. "No, 'nice' isn't the right word. It was fantastic. Marvelous." His grin widened with each word. "*You're* marvelous."

Leaning close, she kissed him. She could say the same about him. Never before had making love with a man seemed so perfect. "You know, I always thought sex was something I could do without. Since I've met you..." She hesitated, not sure she wanted him to know the effect he had on her.

"Yes," he prodded. "Since you met me, what?"

She laughed and rubbed her body against his. "I think I could make love with you all day and night and never get enough."

"Good." He caressed one breast with his hand, gently massaging her nipple. "To tell you the truth, for years I thought I had a low sex drive. Maybe I was just putting all my energy into my work. Maybe..." He forgot about reasons. Simply touching Sasha was arousing him. He chuckled. "Maybe I just needed you. The way you make me feel, we may never get out of this bed."

TIME WAS RUNNING SHORT when they did get out of bed to shower and dress for dinner. While Sasha was in the bathroom, Ross called his parents. He was talking to his mother when Sasha came out. "We'll be back sometime tomorrow afternoon," he said into the mouthpiece. "I'll tell her."

"Tell me what?" Sasha asked as soon as he'd hung up the phone. She'd put on clean underwear, and on the bed lay the dress she would wear to dinner. Elegant but demure, the rose taffeta's neckline was low enough to be fashionable, yet high enough for her to feel comfortable.

"I'm to tell you that you're a lovely woman and that my mother thoroughly enjoyed talking to you."

"I enjoyed talking to her." Sasha slipped the dress over her head and slid her arms into the full sleeves. "How's Jenny doing?"

By the time the skirt's hem reached her ankles, Ross was behind her, ready to help. "Fine, I guess." He pulled up the zipper, then kissed the back of her neck. "Mom put her on the phone so I could talk to her. It gets very frustrating not having her answer, but Mom said she started smiling as soon as she heard my voice. Mom also kept repeating that Jenny's been fine. I hope she's telling me the truth. This is what the doctors said I needed to do. Still, I feel a little guilty."

Turning to face him, Sasha cradled his face in her hands and rose on her tiptoes to tenderly kiss his lips. He had his underpants back on but nothing more. He smelled musky and male, and the memory of his body against hers—in hers—was still very fresh in her mind. "I probably shouldn't have asked you to come with me, to leave her . . . but I'm glad I did."

He returned her kiss, then chuckled. "I said I felt 'a little' guilty, not a lot. I'm glad I came. Today has been . . ." Again he kissed her. "Today has been more than words could describe."

His hands glided over her back and slender waist, and his next kiss was more intense. Sasha pulled her head back, laughing lightly. "Ross Hammond, someone from Benson Toys is going to be at this hotel in a half hour, ready to take us to dinner. Are you planning on going in a pair of blue briefs?"

"Maybe," he said, but he did release his hold and step back. His gaze caressed her face and body, then reluctantly he looked toward the bathroom. "I suppose I'd better take a shower and get dressed. Why don't you call your folks? Tomorrow we could drive across the Bay and stop in and see them. We'll have time. I told Mom not to expect us until afternoon."

"I, ah..." Sasha turned away from Ross and stared into her suitcase. "My folks..." She wasn't sure how to explain her relationship with her parents. "They, ah..."

Quickly she thought up an excuse. "They won't be home tomorrow. They're out of town. Now, where did I put my makeup?"

"It's on the glass table." Her stammering had him curious, but time was too short to ask more about her parents. He really did need to hurry and shower if he was going to be ready on time.

DINNER WAS AN EXTENSION of the publicity hype Benson Toys was structuring around Sasha. From the moment their chauffeur-driven limousine let them off at Fisherman's Wharf, a photographer hovered around Sasha, taking her picture with the Golden Gate Bridge in the background, with the regal old three-masted sailing ship, the *Balclutha*, behind her and with her tentatively holding up a live crab.

Benjamin Bernstein had reserved a private room at the restaurant and had invited Benson Toys's board of directors, important stockholders and members of the press. Sasha was questioned about how she'd started making dolls, how she'd come up with the design for what would now be known as the Victorian Friends, and why she thought dolls were important for children. She answered each question with an ease Ross admired.

He found himself shuffled into the background but didn't mind. This was her night. Standing by the bar that had been set up in the room, a martini in his hand, he watched and listened as Sasha enchanted the men and women standing around her. He could understand the media's fascination with her. The Doll Lady was unique.

"She's perfect," Benjamin Bernstein said, coming over to stand beside Ross. "Did you see these?"

He handed Ross contact prints of the pictures taken earlier that day. They showed Sasha looking into the camera as she faked a signing of the contract, as she examined one of the dolls and as she talked to a worker along the bogus assembly line. Her Victorian-style dress added a special touch to the shots, her smile exuded warmth and her eyes sparkled.

"She alone could sell thousands of these dolls. Mothers listening to her would want to buy one for their children; fathers would drool over her. Actually we'll have to be careful, play down her figure. Don't want any domestic fights started over her."

"I don't think Sasha's interested in being your spokesperson," Ross said.

Bernstein didn't seem perturbed. "Oh, I know she turned down our offer this afternoon, but I don't think she really realizes how much money we're talking. Two years with us and she wouldn't have to work another day in her life. It's an opportunity of a lifetime."

"She likes making dolls and telling stories to children."

Bernstein turned and looked at Ross. "You're her lawyer. Make sure she understands what she's turning down. These pictures show how good she'd be. She could practically write her own contract." He chuckled. "She should like that. She practically wrote her last contract—with your help, of course."

Ross sipped his martini. He didn't know what to say. The offer Benson Toys was making was fantastic. "You're only talking about two years?"

"That's all. Oh, maybe one or two appearances per year, after that. But the big push on this doll will be the first year. After that, we hope it will become a standard—like Barbie dolls."

"Why this doll?" Ross asked, curious.

Bernstein was ready with an answer. "Marketing research has shown that the public is growing tired of highly computerized toys, that there's a trend back to old-fashioned toys that will stimulate a child's imagination. They've also found that children seem to relate better to dolls made of cloth than to smoother, colder, plastic dolls. Something about the textured feel of the material. As for why we chose Sasha's doll—" he smiled "—money. In addition to the dolls, we'll have a market for a complete line of clothing and accessories."

Ross wondered how far they would take the merchandising. He'd noticed that half of the Saturday-morning shows Jenny watched had tie-ins with toys. "Will there be a television series featuring the Victorian Friends?"

Bernstein didn't answer right away. He was watching Sasha. When he did respond to Ross, his words came slowly, as though he were still thinking out the idea. "Television tie-ins haven't panned out as we'd once thought they would, but if she agrees to be the spokesperson for the Victorian Friends, it might work. You say she likes telling stories to children. That's interesting. I can see her seated on a grassy knoll, the Victorian dolls by her side. Real children—dressed in contemporary

clothes—in front of her. She could start to tell a story,
then a half-hour children's story could be shown." He
nodded to himself. "The ads would continue the idea of
storytelling, using the dolls as the audience. It would be
just the opposite of that talking bear. Yes, it might work."

He walked away, toward his public-relations man, and
Ross had a feeling he'd just set an idea in motion. He
wasn't sure if that was good or bad. The offer they were
making Sasha would be a once-in-a-lifetime opportunity, but it would also mean he'd lose her, at least for two
years. He knew what he wanted, and it wasn't for her to
be the Victorian Friends spokesperson. He finished his
martini and ordered another. This, he had a feeling, was
going to be a very long night.

THEY DIDN'T GET BACK to the St. Francis until after eleven.
Ross was on the edge of being drunk; Sasha was wound
up from meeting so many new people, from having her
picture taken so many times and from the sheer pleasure
of rambling on about her dolls. In the hotel room, as she
undressed, she chattered on and on about the dinner
party, the guests and her dolls. Ross didn't care about the
food they'd been served, the people she'd met or her
dolls. Instead of inhibiting his sex drive, the alcohol he'd
consumed was stimulating it. As more and more of her
luscious figure was revealed, he forgot about Benson
Toys, contracts and Sasha's possible stardom. Quickly
he removed his own clothing and stopped Sasha from
putting on the nightgown she'd packed. Kisses silenced
talk; his body expressed his need.

SHE WOKE EARLY the next morning. Her eyes were gritty
from too little sleep, her mouth tasted like cotton and her
thigh muscles were stiff. But she'd never felt happier.

Gently shaking his shoulder, she roused Ross. A walk on the beach was what she wanted.

They dressed quickly—both putting on the clothes they'd worn the day before—got his car out of the hotel's parking lot, found a shop selling croissants and hot coffee and headed for Ocean Beach. Barefoot, they walked on the sand.

Wild, frothy waves broke just offshore and swished up around their ankles. The air had a salty smell, and a cool wind whipped through their hair, blew Sasha's dress around her legs and flattened Ross's shirt against his chest. In companionable silence they walked toward Seal Rocks and ate their breakfast. Occasionally a jogger or other walkers passed them.

She tried to enjoy the coffee she'd doctored with cream and sugar, but after two gulps tossed it out onto the sand. Sea gulls swooped to check whether she'd left anything to eat, squawked their displeasure at finding nothing but wet sand and again rose into the air to continue their search for food.

Sasha danced ahead of Ross. She loved the feel of the sand between her toes, the cool ocean breeze against her cheeks. "This is living!" she cried back to him.

Laughing, he jogged after her. He had to admit she was right. He'd never felt so alive.

It was ten o'clock before they returned to the hotel. Ross grabbed Sasha the moment he closed the door to their room. Pressing her against the wall with his body, he held her with a long kiss, then whispered, "Know what I'd like to do?"

"What?"

"Make love to you."

She kissed the side of his mouth. "Sounds good to me."

"Standing here."

Her eyebrows rose.

"Under your dress."

"Oh, yeah." The idea excited her.

"Both of us fully clothed." He began to pull her long skirt up so it passed her knees and bunched at the meeting of their hips. "Or at least almost fully clothed."

"Almost?" she repeated, and placed her hands on his sides, spanning his ribs. Through his shirt she could feel the heat of his body and the rapid beat of his heart. "And how do you propose to accomplish this feat?" Her fingers moved up and down in a tickling motion.

"I won't—" he laughed, jerking back "—if you keep that up."

"Ross Hammond, you're ticklish."

"Not in the least," he lied, but when she again wiggled her fingers, he pulled completely away from her touch, letting her skirt fall back to her ankles.

"Yes, you are." She found the knowledge delightful. "Now why didn't I realize that before?"

"Maybe because before you've always been a kind, loving lady," he mumbled. At the moment she reminded him of his sister. Ann had relished knowing he was ticklish. It had given her power, and she'd used it to torment him.

His gaze traveled over Sasha. No, she didn't remind him of his sister, but she did have a power over him that was frightening. And she was tormenting him. He still wanted her.

And she wanted him. The tickling had been an accident. It was fun to know that a wiggle of her finger could put him at arm's length, but she preferred him closer. "Come here," she cajoled, her voice pitched low. Slowly she lifted her skirt.

His eyes took in the view of her long legs and the lacy scrap of nothing she wore as panties. She'd put on neither panty hose nor a petticoat that morning and looked more enticing than he'd ever fantasized.

"Oh, Sasha. I'm your slave." Submissively he dropped to his knees in front of her.

They were slaves to each other, to a need that begged to be satisfied. Her command was simple. "Make love to me, Ross."

"Willingly." Placing his hands on her hips, he leaned forward and kissed her.

She drew in a deep breath and tightened her hold on the material of her dress. Looking down, all she could see was the top of his head and his back. What she could feel was another matter. The warmth of his breath. The pressure of his lips and moistness of his tongue. He was turning the entire area between her legs to liquid fire.

"Do you like?" He rubbed his fingers over the swollen mound that so enticed him, felt her arch toward his touch, then slipped his fingers under the wisp of material. She was moist, sweet smelling and very warm. Slowly he let his fingers enter her.

"Do I like?" she repeated, closing her eyes in pure ecstasy. "Oh, yes, I do like."

"So do I." He pulled her panties down, past her knees to her ankles and then off. Then he again touched her, kissed and licked her, delighting in the knowledge that he was bringing her pleasure.

Her entire body was trembling with anticipation when he stood. His eyes were a dark, sultry blue, and his lips tasted of her when he kissed her mouth. She felt him loosen his button and zipper and felt him hard and hot against her as soon as he'd pushed his trousers and shorts down. "Just let the skirt go," he murmured, pressing his hips closer.

She did, moving her hands to his chest and keeping her eyes on his face. He was looking at her, smiling, all the while slowly, rhythmically, moving his hips. She knew she was pleasing him. And as he rubbed against her, stimulating her, he pleased her.

"Think we could have done this last night, in a corner of the room, with all those people around?" He caressed her breasts with his hands.

"At the party Bernstein put on?" Her breathing was ragged.

"I wanted to." His thrusting actions were having the desired effect. He angled himself another way. "Oh, how I wanted to."

She parted her legs a little more, and her hands traveled up to his neck. "I think we would have shocked a few people."

"I'm sure we would have." He pressed hard against her and found the moist warmth he was seeking. With a sigh he closed his eyes. "Oh, yes."

His kiss completed the union. They were one, in reality and in fantasy. He moved inside her, with her, as a part of her. Pressed back against the wall, she let her own eyes close and imagined Ross pulling her away from the newspaper reporters, taking her to a corner of the restaurant's banquet room and making love to her as he was now. She could picture the expression on Benjamin Bernstein's face; on the reporters' faces. It was something she'd never do, but it was fun to imagine. Exciting. Stimulating.

To her surprise, she came before Ross did.

"Good, good," he responded, using her climax to bring his own.

At last, when both were completely satisfied, he drew away and let her skirt hem drop back to her ankles. "Now that's what I'd call a satisfying conclusion to a walk on the beach."

"That's a satisfying conclusion to a lot of things," she said and, wrapping her arms around him, kissed his lips. "You're crazy. . . but fun." Again she kissed him, cuddling close. "Lots of fun."

BY CHECKOUT TIME they'd taken a shower, were dressed and ready to leave for Sacramento. Jenny was ecstatic when she saw her father. Brown curls bobbing, she ran to him, wrapped her arms around his neck and buried her face in his shoulder. No sounds came from her small body, but her joy was contagious, and Sasha found herself wiping a tear from her eyes.

"She really was fine while you two were gone," Ross's mother insisted, coming up beside Sasha. "Oh, a little down right after you left and again this morning when she realized you weren't back, but most of the time she played or helped me around the house. So how did it go in the City?"

"Sasha's a regular celebrity," Ross answered, picking Jenny up as he stood. "She had newspaper reporters writing down every word she said, cameramen taking her picture every time she turned around, and Benson Toys begging her to go to work for them."

Ross's father came up beside his son and teasingly tickled his granddaughter's leg. Jenny pulled her leg away, pushed at her grandfather's hand and grinned, but didn't make a sound. The elder Hammond looked at Jenny's doll, then at Sasha. "When my daughter, Ann, bought that doll, she said there was something special about it. How's it feel to be famous?"

"I'm not famous," denied Sasha.

"She could be, though," Ross argued. "They want her to be the spokesperson for the dolls. They're even talking about giving her a television show."

"And I said no."

Ross wanted her to realize she could still change her mind. "Bernstein said to take a week and think about it."

"Why wouldn't you want to do it?" Ross's father questioned.

"Because it doesn't interest me." One day of being a "star" had been enough.

"Do you really understand what they were offering you?" asked Ross. "It's a once-in-a-lifetime opportunity. Bernstein told me himself that you could write your own contract."

"Ross, I don't want to do it," Sasha said firmly.

"You'd have more money than you'd ever need."

"I don't want the money."

Ross's father frowned. "Maybe the money doesn't sound good to you now, but believe me, my dear, when you're older, you'll appreciate it."

It all sounded so familiar. For years she'd heard the same rhetoric from her father. Over and over he'd said she lived in a dreamworld, that in the real world a person had to make money to survive and that only a fool, an idiot, a simpleminded bumpkin, would waste her time making dolls. For years she'd been told she had no ambition, was worthless, stupid, hopeless. And now Ross and his parents were saying the same thing, were implying that she was a fool not to take the offer. Angry and upset, she clenched her fists and lifted her chin. "I'm not going to do it!"

There was a sudden silence as Jenny, Ross, his mother and father simply stared at Sasha.

"I'm sorry. Please, let's drop the subject."

"So where did you have dinner last night?" Ross's mother finally asked, changing the subject.

"At Fisherman's Wharf," answered Ross, his eyes still on Sasha. Only once before had he heard her raise her voice—that time she'd demanded he stop yelling at Jenny. Now, again, soft-spoken, quiet Sasha Peters had erupted. This was a side to her he didn't understand.

On the drive back to Putnam, just before they arrived at Sasha's house, Ross again brought up the subject of her being a spokesperson for the dolls. "You do realize it would only be for two years, that they'd pay you a tremendous salary and a percentage of the doll sales, don't you?"

She gazed at the willows along the banks of the Yuba River. Emotionally drained, she murmured her answer. "I do."

"Are you afraid to do it? If so, you shouldn't be. You were great yesterday. I saw the contact prints. Bernstein's right. Your smile alone would sell those dolls."

She looked at him. "I'm not afraid, but I'm not going to do it."

"Why?" He needed to know.

"Ross, I know you can't understand this, but I am what I want to be. I'm the Doll Lady. I make dolls, marionettes and hand puppets. I tell children stories. I'm happy with my life as it is."

He considered what she'd said. Her life seemed very insular. "You want nothing more?"

"Nothing money can buy."

"How about marriage?"

9

"MARRIAGE?" Sasha repeated.

"To me. With me." Ross quickly glanced her way, then back at the road. The idea had been bouncing around in his mind all day. Logic warned him that he was rushing things, but he couldn't remember ever being happier, more stimulated or content with a woman. He loved her and he wanted to spend the rest of his life with her. It was as simple as that.

Sasha didn't answer immediately but turned to look at Jenny. The little girl's eyes were closed, her head was tilted to the side. The twists and turns of Highway 49 had put her to sleep; she wasn't aware of the conversation going on in the front seat.

Finally Sasha's gaze returned to rest on Ross's profile. A sickening knot was forming in her stomach. "Let me get this straight. You're asking me to marry you?"

"Yes." Again his attention left the road as he tried to gauge her reaction to the idea. "I love you and want to marry you."

"Ross, you hardly know me."

"I know you well enough. I know you're a warm, giving person. A sweet, sexy woman." He chuckled, grinning. "I know you're a hell of a lover."

She shook her head. "One night in a hotel room isn't enough to base a marriage proposal on."

"I'm not. I've known you for two months now. For the last few weeks we've been working side by side. I like being around you. It's not just sex I'm looking for."

"Ross, you don't really know me. You're jumping into this just like you did the first time you got married."

"My asking you to marry me in no way resembles my proposal to Donna." He was upset that Sasha would even make the comparison.

"Well, I can tell you for certain I wouldn't be any good for your career. I love living here in the mountains, in a small community. I couldn't go back to living in the city, and I wouldn't be a good hostess."

"I don't need a hostess, and I'm not going back to the city. Sasha, when I first met you, I didn't think I knew how to love. Now I'm ready to punch out every guy who looks at you with more than a passing interest. I'm happy when I'm around you, miserable when I'm not. I love you, and I think you love me."

She looked out the side window. Did she love him? What was love? She would admit that his kisses were different from the kisses she'd shared with other men, and that their lovemaking had been special—very special. But love? Marriage? She thought of her mother... then her father. Involuntarily she shivered.

Sasha wasn't saying anything, and Ross felt he had to. "We get along well. We like a lot of the same things."

"As I recall, I don't hold a hammer right, don't remember to put my tools back where they belong, and have a weird taste in music."

"Minor problems. I'm talking about philosophies of life. We want the same things: honest relationships, simple pleasures."

She glanced his way. His knuckles were white where he was gripping the steering wheel, and his mouth was a tense line. He was worried. Well, so was she.

"Ross, you're going through a lot of changes right now, and a lot of stress. Whether you loved her or not, the woman you'd lived with for five years died, you almost lost your daughter, you've changed jobs, moved. And you're still worried about Jenny—about her ever talking again and about her emotional adjustment. I'm someone different from the women you've known before. With me, around me, you're learning to relax, learning to enjoy life. I think you *think* you love me. Actually it's probably gratitude."

He headed down the steep drive to her house. Some of what she'd said was true. He was going through a lot of changes. But he knew that what he felt for Sasha was not gratitude. Or, at least, it wasn't *just* gratitude. He stopped in front of her place, switched off the engine and turned in his seat to face her.

"Sure, I'm grateful to you. And you are different from the women I've known, but gratitude is not all I feel for you. Sasha, I love you, and I want to marry you."

"I can't," she said, and started to unsnap her seat belt.

Ross put his hand over hers. He felt as though something were dying inside. "You can't get married? Or you can't love me?"

"All I ever wanted was to be your friend." Tears were forming in her eyes, and she wanted to get away. She pulled her hand free from his, the seat belt falling aside as she did.

"I don't understand you. After what we shared, I thought—"

"No, you don't understand me," she agreed. He didn't know how many hours she'd spent locked in her room because her father "loved" her. He didn't know all the cruel things her father had said to her when she was growing up, all in the name of "love." Ross didn't know, and she couldn't tell him because it was something she'd never been able to talk about. "I'm just sorry. I never meant for this to happen."

"Sorry?" He couldn't believe she was passing off his proposal so casually.

Nero and Polo ran up to the car, barking, tails wagging. Both jumped up on Ross's side, scratching at the car's finish with their sharp toenails. In the back seat Jenny woke, looked around and started to unfasten her seat belt.

"Damn those dogs!" snapped Ross, his frustration turning on them. "Do you have any idea how much a new paint job on one of these cars costs?"

Moving forward, Jenny reached between the seats and pulled on his sleeve.

He switched his attention to her.

She made a series of gestures, but he couldn't understand what she wanted. "Dammit all, Jenny, why don't you talk?"

"Ross Hammond, don't yell at her," demanded Sasha. "Don't terrorize *her* with your love." She opened her door. "I'll get the dogs away from your precious car."

She called to Nero and Polo, and they loped around the front bumper, eager to greet her. Numb and confused, Ross watched for a second, then looked back at Jenny. With wide blue eyes, she was staring at him.

Sasha was right. There was no reason for him to jump all over his daughter just because he was upset. "I'm sorry," he mumbled. Then, not knowing what else to do, he leaned over and pushed the button to open the trunk.

As he went to get Sasha's suitcase, Jenny climbed to the front seat and then out of the car.

"Thanks for going with me." Sasha's voice was a monotone, her posture stiff as she stood waiting for him.

Mechanically Ross opened the trunk and pulled out her suitcase, but he held on to the handle so she couldn't take it. "We've got to talk about this."

"There's nothing to talk about."

"Yes, there is. What about us? What now?"

She looked down at the ground, at the toe of her white pumps and the hem of her skirt. She didn't really have an answer. Slowly her gaze moved back up to his face. "I don't know. I'd still like to be your friend."

"It's not enough."

"It's all I can handle."

For a second he stared at her face, then shook his head and handed her the suitcase.

As he turned away, she called out his name.

Pausing, he looked back. "What?"

"I—" She didn't know what to say. "Thank you . . . for everything."

Again he shook his head. He was too confused to know what to think. That morning he'd felt like a king; the day had been perfect. Now, all he wanted to do was crawl off and lick his wounds. Jenny was heading for the goat pen. Ross yelled for her to get back into the car, and when she didn't come, he followed her, scooped her up under an arm and carried her back to the car.

There were tears in the child's eyes when Ross pulled out of Sasha's yard. He ignored them and stared straight ahead, glancing only once in the rearview mirror. Sasha hadn't moved from where she stood, suitcase in hand, the dogs by her side. When he turned onto the highway, he had the urge to step on the accelerator and roar into oblivion. Instead, he kept to a steady speed and headed for his house. Life would go on, he told himself. He'd survived thirty-three years without Sasha. She was right. They'd known each other only a short time. Maybe what he was feeling was simply gratitude. Maybe he really didn't know what love was.

He felt a tear slip down his cheek and rubbed it away with the back of his hand. Dammit all, life was unfair.

He knew what love was, all right; only the woman he loved didn't love him.

OVER AND OVER Sasha told herself she'd done the right thing, that it was better to end her relationship with Ross as she had than to let it continue and be hurt. Only she did hurt. Deep inside. The ache simply wouldn't go away. No matter what she did, she felt miserable.

On Tuesday she found a dead bird and burst into tears. She blamed her moodiness on the weather and the time of the month, but deep down she knew why the tears had come so easily and that it wasn't a fallen junco she was mourning.

Wednesday, Ross brought Jenny to story hour. Jenny immediately joined the group of children already on the rug, and Sasha found her gaze locked with Ross's. He looked tired, haggard. It bothered her to know she was responsible for the dark circles under his eyes, and she looked away. When she glanced back, he was gone.

Jenny didn't seem to mind her father's absence, and by the end of the story hour he'd returned. Without a word, he took Jenny's hand and left the library.

He didn't come out to the house at all that week, and Sasha had a feeling Never-Neverland had become just that for him—a place he'd *never* return to. After having worked beside him for so many days, she had to admit his absence created a void.

That weekend was Memorial Day, and she was scheduled to put on two puppet shows in Downieville. She hoped being busy would keep her mind off Ross. It didn't.

One thing Memorial Day weekend did was herald the beginning of summer. And summer meant change for Sasha. For the past two years Putnam's town council, in connection with the library, had hired her to run a special program over the summer months. Two mornings a week—weather permitting—the town's park became the center for storytelling, puppet making and other crafts and creative activities.

Children of all ages came, including the preschoolers, and Sasha ended her Wednesday-morning story hours until school started again. As a celebration for those who would be leaving the story-hour group and starting kindergarten in the fall, Sasha planned a party at her house. One by one she called the parents of all the children who had attended her story hour during the year and issued her invitation. She left the call to Jenny's house until the last.

As she dialed Ross's number, her hands turned clammy and butterflies invaded her stomach. Shaking inside, barely able to breathe, she waited for him to answer. When she heard his voice, her throat went incredibly dry and it was almost impossible for her to speak. With a rasp she issued the invitation to bring Jenny to her place instead of the library on Wednesday morning.

"Sasha, I miss you," he said quietly.

"I miss you, too," she admitted, her heart thudding in her ears.

"Does that mean you've changed your mind?"

Closing her eyes, she said nothing. Had she changed her mind? She was miserable without him, but she feared she'd be even more miserable with him.

"Sasha, are you still there?" he asked after a long silence.

"Yes," she whispered. "I mean, no, I haven't changed my mind. I'm sorry, Ross, but I can't ever be more than a friend to you."

He hung up without another word.

Tuesday afternoon she bought the fixings for the party and spent the evening baking cookies—her house taking on the mouthwatering aromas of chocolate, vanilla and peanut butter. Food, however, had lost its appeal, and she didn't even snitch bites of the freshly baked treats. Since her return from San Francisco, she had eaten little.

On Wednesday morning the cars began to arrive just before eleven. Nero and Polo were delighted to have so many people to investigate and entertain. Sasha kept watching for a silver-and-black BMW. When Jenny got out of Mandy's mother's car, Sasha knew he wasn't coming.

"Ross asked if I'd mind bringing Jenny," Ruth explained. "It's the least I could do. He's helped me so much lately." Tears filled the petite brunette's eyes. "I'm leaving Carl."

Sasha knew then what woman had been talking to Ross about a divorce.

Blinking and wiping at her eyes with a tissue, Ruth managed a wan smile. "He's a wonderful man, Sasha. Absolutely wonderful."

"Carl?"

"No, Ross. He's so understanding."

"Yes, he is, isn't he?" Sasha tried to sound enthusiastic but couldn't. Ruth's admiring statements were too heartfelt, too adoring. A jealousy she'd never known before gnawed at Sasha's insides. She hurried to get the party going for the children.

For the rest of the week, as she finished redecorating the spare bedroom, Sasha kept wondering just how understanding Ross was. The time Ruth had brought Mandy to Jenny's tea party, she'd grumbled that her husband hadn't slept with her for weeks. And, as Sasha recalled, Ruth had openly admired Ross's good looks.

So what? Why should you care if he's sleeping with her? You told him it was over, didn't you? Sasha ham-

mered away at the nails with a vengeance, her hand on
the handle the way she liked, not the way Ross had suggested. *You're better off without him! Men only want to
boss. Control. Men—*

She hit her thumb and the tears came. Sitting down on
the floor, sucking on her injured thumb, she cried.

By July, Sasha was sure she had her emotions under
control. It helped that she rarely saw Ross. Jenny was
coming to the Tuesday and Thursday programs, but it
was Ruth who brought her, along with Mandy. Jenny still
didn't talk, but she was becoming more robust and out-
going every week.

Besides the park program and the work on her house,
Sasha was trying to come up with a new doll concept to
replace the My Friends dolls. During the second week in
July she went to the hospital in Grass Valley to entertain
the children. Her puppets and stories brought smiles to
pale faces, and she thought of Jenny... and Ross. He'd
told her how they'd used Anna to help Jenny recuperate.

After her performance Sasha had lunch with some of
the doctors and nurses. They were delighted with one of
the puppets she'd brought. The wooden marionette,
which had a removable cast, had started out hobbling
and ended up dancing.

"Kids need to know they're not the only one in the
world with an injury and that someday the cast or bandages will come off," one nurse said. "That puppet was
just what they needed to see."

So Sasha left it with her and on the drive back to Putnam came up with an idea for a new doll.

Working on the design helped keep her mind off the
emptiness she still felt with Ross no longer around. For
the next two weeks she created a variety of modeled
heads, arms and legs until she found a combination she

liked, then she experimented with the body. What she wanted were dolls that were lovable and cuddly, but could be used by the doctors and nurses to help a child understand what was wrong or what was going to happen. That meant the dolls had to be anatomically correct, to the point of including internal organs that could be seen by pulling apart a Velcro closing.

Once she had a design that satisfied her, she worked on the accessories. She needed to come up with casts for the arms and legs, body casts, neck braces and bandages. She experimented with a variety of materials. Each item needed to be realistic looking, safe for small children to handle, and easy to clean. When she was satisfied with her results, Sasha took her designs and ideas to the hospital and showed them to the staff. By the time she left, she had an order for a dozen dolls.

Which was good. She needed the money. Over two months had passed since she'd signed the contract with Benson Toys, and she still hadn't seen any cash. She had a feeling something was wrong but couldn't guess what, and she didn't want to believe there really was a problem.

Benjamin Bernstein had called at the end of June to ask again if she'd be interested in helping to promote the Victorian Friends. He'd been so enthusiastic then, telling her about the publicity blitz they'd done with the pictures they took while she was in San Francisco, how their salesmen had all fallen in love with her, and what great hopes they had for the dolls. Then two weeks ago he'd called again to ask if she'd copied the doll from someone else's design. She'd quickly assured him that she hadn't. And he'd laughed when she asked why and said not to worry, that she'd be getting her money soon. She hadn't, though, and she was becoming concerned. Nevertheless, she hadn't called or gone to see Ross.

She was reluctant to face him. She hadn't been able to pay him back what she owed him, and she wished she could. Without income from the My Friends dolls, she was behind in paying several of her bills, and it was only the summer program at the park and her occasional show at a hospital or community center that were keeping the creditors off her back.

When Benjamin Bernstein called two days later, she prayed it was to say her check was in the mail.

It wasn't.

After she hung up, all she could do was sit and stare at the telephone. The bottom had dropped out of her world. Not only would she not be getting the money she'd expected, she might lose everything she had. The last thing Bernstein had said was "You'd better talk to that lawyer of yours."

Finally lifting the receiver, she started to dial Ross's number, then changed her mind. Ten minutes later she stood in front of the side door to Ross's home. His name was on a brass plate attached to the siding, a reversible sign that said Open—Come In on one side and Closed—Please Call for an Appointment on the other hanging below it. The Open side was forward, and Sasha turned the knob and stepped inside.

The room she entered held four chairs, several file cabinets, a painting of the Sierra Buttes with Upper Sardine Lake in the foreground, and a large desk. Ruth was sitting behind the desk, sorting through a folder of papers. She looked up and smiled at Sasha.

"Hi. What a surprise to see you here. Did you want to see Ross?" Ruth glanced through the open door to his office. "He just went upstairs to get something the girls wanted from the closet. He'll be back down in a minute."

"I . . ." Sasha didn't know what to say or do. An invisible knife was twisting in her stomach.

She hadn't heard that Ruth was working for Ross . . . living with him. But then she'd been so busy working on the new dolls that she hadn't been around people to hear the gossip.

"I . . ." Again she tried, but the words wouldn't come. Turning away, Sasha caught her lower lip between her teeth and headed for the outside door.

She couldn't talk to Ross. Not now, not today. Things were too confusing. She needed time to think, time to work out her feelings.

Sasha was halfway to her car when Ross called her name. She was tempted to pretend she hadn't heard and to keep going, but she knew he wouldn't believe it and that she'd be acting like a fool if she didn't turn around. Stopping, she slowly faced him.

"What did you want?" he asked, his heart in his throat. When he'd returned to his office and was told that Sasha had just left, he couldn't believe his ears. Staring at her, he couldn't believe his eyes. She looked wonderful and she looked terrible. There were circles under her eyes and she'd lost too much weight, but never had he seen a woman he wanted more.

"I . . ." The words still wouldn't come. She didn't know where to begin. Shoulders slumped, she looked down at her feet. "Bernstein called."

"And?" Ross walked toward her. Her posture and expression said it wasn't good news.

She looked up, her pulse pounding in her ears, and watched him approach. "He said there's a man . . . a man in New York who claims he's the originator of the Friends dolls. This man, he . . . he said I copied his design."

Ross stopped directly in front of her, and Sasha stared into his eyes. They seemed bluer than she remembered.

Kinder. Warmer. She longed to step into his arms and be held tight. She wanted to hear him tell her everything would be all right, for him to run his fingers through her hair, to murmur sweet words into her ear and kiss her lips. It took all her strength to stand where she was and go on with her explanation.

"He—this man—saw the pictures of me holding the doll and called Benson Toys. He says he's got pictures and documents showing he was making and selling dolls exactly like mine twelve years ago. *Exactly* like mine," she repeated for emphasis. "He claims I copied him."

"And did you?"

"No. Of course not. I wouldn't do such a thing."

"And what did Bernstein say?"

"That the guy's threatening to sue Benson Toys—and me. That they can't pay me a cent until they know I'm the true creator of the doll. That I'd better see you right away."

Ross whistled through his teeth and studied her. He wanted to take her into his arms but didn't. She looked vulnerable and delectable, but what she needed right now was legal help, not him trying to convince her that they should be together. Those desires would have to wait. Stepping to the side, he motioned toward his office door. "Come on back inside. I'd like to call and talk to Bernstein myself."

Sasha hesitated. "Ruth said you were busy with the girls."

"Mandy just wanted me to get a game from the top shelf. All's taken care of."

"Ruth is, ah, that is . . ." She wasn't quite certain how to ask if Ruth was living with him.

"She's been working for me for two weeks now. She needed a job but hated the idea of leaving Mandy with a sitter. This is working out quite well. The girls entertain each other, and one of us is usually available if it's necessary to get something for them."

In a small town like Putnam she couldn't avoid the reality of Ross living with another woman. Although she was dying inside, she tried to sound congenial. "That's nice . . . for both of you. I'm . . . I'm glad you found someone."

When they came through the door, Ruth looked up from the paper she'd been typing and again smiled. "You caught her, I see."

"Just barely." Ross glanced at his watch. "Do I have any more appointments today?"

"The Harters wanted to talk to you about setting up a college trust fund for their son."

Ross grinned. "The baby's only two months old. I think we have time. Please call them and reschedule the appointment."

He closed the door between his office and Ruth's. The door that led to his house, however, stayed open, and Sasha could hear Mandy's voice in the other room. As usual, the little girl was issuing orders. Ross nodded toward the sound. "That child's so bossy I sometimes wish Jenny would tell her to go jump in the lake."

"Jenny's talking?" She hadn't heard her say anything while at the park.

He shook his head. "Not a word. I've been taking her to see a doctor in Grass Valley, but it doesn't seem to be helping." Sitting behind his desk, he picked up his telephone, flipped through a Rolodex until he came to the name he wanted and dialed a number.

"Sit down. Relax," he encouraged Sasha. She looked tense and worried. He was glad to see her again, but not like this. "I want to hear what Bernstein has to say. Then we'll figure out what to do."

She did sit down, and while Ross talked on the telephone, she studied him.

He looked as great as ever to her. More tanned. Maybe a little leaner. He wasn't wearing a jacket and his short-sleeved cotton shirt and slacks mimicked the casual attire most of Putnam's businessmen adopted during the summer months. His hair was longer than the first time she'd seen him, now curling against his neck and just over his ears. She longed to run her fingers through it. Instead she folded her hands in her lap and stared out the window by his desk.

"Don't worry about it, Ben," Ross finished. "I'm sure we can straighten this whole thing out in no time."

Hanging up, he looked at Sasha. "You haven't received any money from Benson Toys?"

"No. If I had, I would have paid you." She felt guilty. He'd done so much for her already and hadn't received a cent.

"I'm not worried about your paying me. I am worried about this man in New York. As I recall, you never got a patent or copyright on your doll design."

"I never thought of it—not until you mentioned it. And you said then that Benson Toys would do it."

"They've applied for one. I wish you had, but at least it seems that this guy didn't, either. What we need to do now is prove that you created the doll first. When did you start selling the My Friends dolls?"

"I sold my first one when I was eighteen." She still remembered that sale. She'd been afraid she had priced the doll too high, that no one would pay seventy-five dollars for a cloth doll; but the woman had called it a bargain and a month later had ordered another.

"Ten years ago." Ross shook his head. "Our New Yorker says he created his and had it on the market twelve years ago, and that he can prove it. He'll claim you saw one of his and copied it, even if you didn't."

"Lots of people make Victorian-type dolls."

"With navels, dimples on the bottom and eyes like these dolls have?"

"Well, maybe not, but even if I did see one of his, I've been making them for more than ten years."

"How much longer?"

"I made the first one when I was ten."

That sounded good to him. "Can you prove it?"

"How do you mean prove it?"

"Do you have any photographs of you holding the doll when you were ten?"

She shook her head. "My father wouldn't let me have my picture taken with a doll."

Ross's eyebrows rose. "Why not?"

"He hated dolls—said if girls would stop playing with dolls, they'd have more time to learn about the important things in life."

"Your father said that?"

"Often." Until it was etched in her mind. Still, it hadn't stopped her from wanting a doll.

"So there are no photos of your first doll." Elbows on his desktop, he clasped his hands and leaned his chin on entwined fingers. "What about those hospital benefits you did? Would people remember seeing your dolls there?"

"Probably, but I didn't start doing them until after I was eighteen. I wasn't allowed—"

She stopped, and Ross was curious. "You weren't allowed what?"

It was difficult for her to talk about her childhood. Sasha tried to find the right words to explain. "I never did any hospital benefits when I lived at home. My father didn't approve of giving away one's time."

Ross was beginning to wonder about her father. "Any friends who saw this doll? People who could testify in court that you were making them when you were ten or eleven?"

She shook her head. "No."

After her father destroyed the first doll, she'd hid the others in a trunk and taken them out only when she knew it was safe. "Some of my teachers saw the designs when I first started creating the dolls." She chuckled. "I used to make sketches of them on my papers until—"

Again she stopped and Ross had to prompt her. "Until?"

She sighed. "Until they mentioned it to Dad." He'd been furious, and she'd been grounded for a month.

"I don't suppose you have any of those old school papers with the drawings on them just lying around."

"Not unless Mom kept them." It was a possibility. "She always kept everything Tanya and I did."

"Why don't you call and ask if she has them?" He nodded toward the telephone on his desk.

"Now?" Sasha glanced at the clock on his wall. It showed just past two. Actually it would be safe. Her dad wouldn't be home yet. She could call, but she'd rather not.

"If she's got those papers with those drawings, we'll be free and clear. We'll take them to Bernstein, have copies made and let his lawyers deal with this guy in New York."

"Chances are she doesn't have them." Sasha was sure her father would have had them destroyed—if not when she was young, then after she had left home.

"Nothing gained if we don't try. Give her a call." He couldn't understand her hesitancy and pushed the phone toward her.

"Mom's probably not home."

"Sasha . . ." His curiosity was piqued. "Why are you putting this off?"

"I, ah, well—"

"What kind of a relationship do you have with your family?"

Considering the closeness he shared with his parents, she could understand his questioning her actions. This wasn't going to be easy to explain. "Well, I'm sort of a persona non grata. At least with my father."

Ross frowned. "You're not talking to your father?"

"No. I'd talk to him, but he doesn't want to talk to me."

"And what about your mother?"

"Oh, we get along fine, but Dad won't let her talk to me. Nevertheless, she does. Whenever I call her, that is. And she writes to me, and when I lived in Oakland, she used to sneak over and visit me."

"Sneak?"

Sasha knew she should have picked a better word. "I mean, we'd plan our visits so Dad wouldn't know about them."

"Why won't your father talk to you or let your mother talk to you?"

Why, indeed? It all seemed so stupid. With a sigh Sasha answered. "Because my father banned me. To him, I no longer exist, and he's forbidden my mother to talk to me, see me or even mention my name."

"You're kidding." What she was telling him was bizarre.

"I wish I were." She supposed Ross deserved a more complete explanation. "When I graduated from high school, my father and I had a big argument. He figured I'd go on to college; I couldn't see any sense in it. I knew what I wanted to do, and I didn't know of any college where doll making and storytelling were majors."

"And then?"

"That's it. We argued over college, he told me to get out of his house and stopped talking to me."

It sounded ridiculous to him. "When was the last time you were home?"

"That day we argued." She'd gone to a friend's house that night, had found a job and a place to live the next week, and her mother, against her father's wishes, had brought her things to her.

"So you lied when we were in San Francisco and you said we couldn't go see your folks because they were out of town."

"I lied," she admitted.

"But you do call your mother sometimes."

Sasha nodded. "Whenever I'm sure Dad is at work."

"And is he at work now?"

Again she nodded, and Ross pushed the telephone the last few inches toward her. "Then call your mother. See if she saved any of those papers with the drawings of the doll on them."

10

SASHA PAUSED in her conversation with her mother. "She says she does have a lot of my old school papers stored in boxes and knows some have drawings on them, but she doesn't know if any are drawings of the doll."

"Tell her we'll be down tomorrow to look through them."

"I—" She wasn't sure she wanted to go. The day she left, she'd sworn never to go back.

"Do you want to win this case or not?"

"I want to win." Sasha relayed the message to her mother, talked for a while longer, then hung up. For a second she simply stared at the receiver in its cradle, then slowly sank back in her chair.

Ross could read the concern on her face. "We'll leave early tomorrow, get to your parents' place soon after your father goes to work and be gone long before he comes home."

It sounded easy enough. Experience had taught Sasha that life was never easy. "Mom said Dad has a cold. A cold rarely slows my father down, but I can tell you, Ross, all hell would break loose if we arrived and he was there."

"I'll go to the door first. If he's there... Well, we'll work something out. I've negotiated some pretty tough deals in the past."

She doubted that even Ross could negotiate a deal with her father, but his understanding helped. "I appreciate what you're doing and—"

She was interrupted by a knock on the door, and Ross looked in the direction of the sound. "Yes?"

The door opened a little way and Ruth peeked in. "I've got all of those letters typed and have rescheduled the Harters' appointment for next week. Unless you have something else, I think I'll take Mandy and go home now."

He'd forgotten about Ruth and Mandy. With Sasha sitting in front of him, he'd forgotten everything except her and the problem she now faced. "Before you leave, cancel any appointments I have for tomorrow. I'm going to be out of town." Smiling, he added, "That'll give you a day off to go see Carl."

At the mention of her husband's name, Ruth's expression turned warm and appreciative. "No problem. You only have two."

Again closing the door, Ruth disappeared from their view, and Sasha faced Ross. She was confused. "I thought you two . . . That is . . ." Stopping, she collected her thoughts. "Isn't Ruth living here? With you?"

"With me?" Ross chuckled at the idea and shook his head. "Heavens, no. She did move back with her folks for a while, but now that her husband's in the rehab center, Ruth's back in her own house and they're trying to work out their problems."

His smile vanished and his eyes narrowed. "Sasha, did you really think she was living here?"

She looked down at her lap, hating the jealous thoughts that had plagued her. "I didn't know what to think."

"Are people linking Ruth's name with mine?" He hadn't considered that possibility when he hired her. Malicious gossip wouldn't help Ruth's relationship with her husband.

"I don't think so. I mean, I haven't heard anything. I just thought . . ." She glanced up to explain, then immediately looked back down. She couldn't confess what she'd thought.

He rose from his chair and came around his desk to stand in front of her. "Sasha Peters, look at me."

Slowly she did.

"I guess I didn't state my case well enough the last time we were together. Let me repeat myself. *I love you.*" His precise enunciation of each of the three words left no room for misunderstanding.

He held out his hands, and for a moment she simply stared at them. He loved her. Not Ruth. Not anyone else. Her. And he wanted her to accept that as a fact.

Without consciously making a decision, she reached up and joined her hands with his. Easily he pulled her to her feet. His arms wrapped around her, his lips touched hers, and she sighed. The emptiness she'd felt for so many weeks was replaced by a sense of completeness. Fears were forgotten, jealousy banished.

The kiss might have lasted forever, but the door opened again. "Appointments canceled. I'll—"

Ruth stopped midsentence, and Ross lifted his head but didn't loosen his hold on Sasha. Ruth grinned and continued. "I'll get Mandy now and take off. Do you want me to take Jenny with me? She could spend the night at my place."

Ross considered the idea, but Sasha spoke before he had a chance to answer. "No need for that, Ruth. I'll be leaving in a couple of minutes."

"If you say so." Ruth continued through Ross's office and into the main part of the house toward the living room, where Mandy could still be heard giving instructions to Jenny.

Ross gazed down at Sasha's face. "You don't need to leave, you know."

"Yes, I do." She needed time to think. She cared for Ross more than she'd ever cared for any man. The fact that she couldn't banish him from her thoughts or lessen her desire proved that. Nevertheless, she still didn't know what to do about those feelings.

"I've missed you, you know," he confessed. "The only reason I've stayed away is because you had doubts. You said you thought that what I felt for you was gratitude...or confusion. Well, believe me, it isn't either. I'm not the least bit confused about what I'm feeling, nor am I grateful for the torture you've been putting me through these past few weeks. Still, I love you."

"Ross, you just don't understand. I—"

A quick kiss silenced her. When he lifted his head, he was somber. "I do understand. I don't blame you for worrying about a man who's told you he was a workaholic, but I've got that under control. I know I have. And I realize that telling you I married a woman I didn't love just because it would help my career must have made me sound pretty callous. I'm not proud of that. Still, I'm not going to pretend I'm mourning Donna's death. We had nothing between us. The only good thing that came out of our relationship was Jenny."

He paused and gazed down into Sasha's green eyes. "I know it isn't fair to ask you to marry me and take on a handicapped child. I—"

"Oh, Ross, it's not Jenny, or Donna, or anything you've done." She pulled away from his tender hold. "Don't you understand? I'm the one who's handicapped."

"How?" he demanded, confused. "What's your handicap, Sasha?"

"Fear."

IT WASN'T AN ANSWER, but when Ross questioned her further, she didn't really elaborate. All Sasha could tell him was that she was afraid of marriage.

Logically she knew she should simply accept his love; but logic had nothing to do with her fears. She'd psychoanalyzed herself and knew the root of her problem was her father. But knowing why she panicked at the idea of a commitment didn't make the anxiety any less real. Sasha left soon after Ruth did.

Ross had been upset with her, and she'd been afraid he'd completely wash his hands of her, tell her she was on her own as far as a lawsuit went. But he called later and told her to be ready early in the morning. The trip was still on.

Soon after the sun came up, she milked the goat and fed the dogs and cat. By the time Ross pulled his BMW into her yard, she was dressed and ready, butterflies dancing in her stomach. Jenny was in the back seat of the car, wearing shorts, sandals and a cotton top, and had Anna and a stack of picture books beside her. Sasha greeted the child with a cheery hello and was rewarded with a big smile and a wave.

Ross wasn't smiling when he slid out from behind the steering wheel and came around to hold open the car door. He greeted her formally, apologizing for having to bring Jenny along. "I couldn't find a baby-sitter I'd trust for the entire day. Even your sister was busy."

"No problem," she said, and lifted her long skirt to step into the car. "Let's just hope you're not wasting your time taking me down there."

"Life's a gamble."

Sasha didn't respond. She knew he was making a point.

At first they talked about mundane matters—her animals, her garden and the weather—then they both fell silent. Ross kept his eyes on the road, and Sasha looked out the side window. She watched a hawk soar on the air currents high above craggy peaks, spotted two deer in the shadow of a grove of cedars and heeded the Watch for Falling Rocks signs. She didn't see any. The two-lane highway twisted and turned as it followed the Yuba River, and so did her mind, turning again and again from thoughts of seeing her mother to Ross. More than once she glanced his way.

He was dressed for the hot weather they'd been having, his white slacks a lightweight cotton blend that hugged his hips and looked casual, his short-sleeved blue-and-white striped shirt unbuttoned partway. His arms were tanned, a few curly tawny-brown hairs showed on his chest and he looked sexy. When she realized the direction her thoughts were traveling, she quickly looked back out the side window. Still, a rush of desire heated her entire body.

Sasha Peters, how can you want a man and not want him at the same time? She had no answer.

They stopped for gas when they reached I-80, and the moment Ross opened the car door, Sasha wished she'd worn shorts instead of her usual long dress. It wasn't quite eight o'clock, but it felt like an oven outside. She hoped it would be cooler in Oakland. The ocean breezes generally kept the Bay Area far more comfortable than the Sacramento Valley.

Once they were on the freeway they made good time. It had been over a year since she'd made the drive from Putnam to Oakland; the golden-brown rolling hills still seemed the same. It wasn't until Ross turned off the freeway that Sasha noticed changes. Ten years had passed since she'd taken the road that led up the Oakland hills to her parents' home. When they drew near, she gave Ross directions by rote. So many of the houses seemed different, and she didn't recognize anyone she saw on the street. Her mother often wrote about the people Sasha had grown up with. Many had moved away. Thank goodness for those letters and calls. She did miss her mother.

Since she'd moved to Putnam, their visits had ended completely. Not even Tanya's wedding had brought Orrie Peters to the vicinity of his younger daughter. There'd been two wedding ceremonies: a small one at the house in Oakland—only the immediate family—sans one— present; the other held in Putnam—the entire town invited and most attending; including Sasha as maid of honor. Sasha had considered two weddings an inconvenience for Tanya and had urged her sister to make their father come to Putnam—she had even offered to disappear for the day to ease tensions—but, as usual, Tanya had tried to please everyone.

Ross parked the BMW in front of the house, angling his tires into the curb because of the steep incline. "I'll go see if the coast is clear."

"No, I'll go up." As long as they were there, she wanted to see her mother, if only until her father told her to leave.

"Then we'll all go." He came around and opened her door and let Jenny out of the back.

Standing on the lawn, Sasha stared at the house that had once been her home. Built on the side of a hill, it was two stories in front, three in back. The red-brick foundation, hunter-green shutters and white wooden siding all looked the same. Fuchsia bushes, neatly trimmed hedges, beds of colorful flowers and a well-manicured lawn gave the house a warm, welcoming appearance. Sasha knew better.

"Ready?" Ross asked by her side.

She jumped at the sound of his voice. Looking into his eyes, she wished she could explain what it had been like growing up in this house—with her father. Too many years of silence kept the words from coming. With a sigh she looked away and took a step toward the front door.

Letters and telephone calls couldn't compare to seeing her mother in person again. Sasha wrapped her arms around the tall, slender woman. "Oh, Mom. It's been too long."

Tears in her eyes, Sasha's mother hugged her daughter. "I should have gone up to see you . . . to see both you and Tanya."

"No, Mom. We know how he would act, how miserable he would make things for you. We understand."

"He just won't go, and he won't let me go alone. He knows if I do, I'll go see you, too. He's so damn stubborn." The older woman sighed, then looked over her daughter's shoulder at Ross and Jenny and smiled. "Sasha, I think introductions are in order."

Sasha quickly introduced Irena Peters to Ross and Jenny, explaining Jenny's accident and lack of speech as briefly as possible. Shyly Jenny stood by Ross, clutching Anna. Sasha's mother knelt in front of the child. "I see you have one of Sasha's dolls. Do you like it?"

Jenny nodded.

Irena Peters looked up at Sasha. "There was an article in the newspaper a few weeks ago about Benson Toys buying the dolls from you. I thought your father might say something about it, but he didn't."

"Nothing?" Sasha had also hoped her success with the dolls might change her father's attitude.

"No. He still won't mention your name." Softly she spoke to Jenny. "Sasha's daddy didn't like her making dolls, but no matter how much he'd rant and rave, Sasha kept on making them. She'd make a doll out of anything. I remember paper dolls, flower dolls, clothespin dolls . . . And one time when I bought some corn on the cob, she made dolls out of corn husks."

Ross spoke up. "And I understand she also made drawings of dolls—drawings of this doll." He pointed to Anna.

Sasha's mother glanced up, then stood, smiling. "Not that one, but ones like it. That is, until her father found out and made her stop."

"If you have any of those drawings, any that would date the doll's creation back to when Sasha was ten or eleven, we need them."

Irena Peters grimaced. "I'm afraid my husband destroyed most of the drawings. I don't know if any are on the papers I kept. I didn't have a chance to look through them last night. Orrie came home soon after we talked." She looked at Sasha. "That cold I mentioned is bothering him. He came home an hour early yesterday."

"But he went to work today?" Sasha was sure he had. Her mother wouldn't be this relaxed if there was a chance Orrie Peters might appear.

"Left at his usual time. Not that he sounded all that good, but you know him. He believes in a day's work for a day's pay. Won't stay home until it turns into pneumonia."

"I do think we should look at those papers right away," Ross said. He'd noticed that Sasha tensed whenever her father was mentioned. He knew she didn't want to run into him.

Sasha's mother's gaze turned to Ross. "The boxes are upstairs in what used to be Tanya's room."

All four of them went up the stairs to the bedroom. From the top shelf of the closet, back behind stacks of linens, Sasha's mother pulled out three cardboard cartons and handed them down to Ross. He set them next to the single bed in the room.

"You'll find both Tanya's and Sasha's papers mixed together and in no real order. I just shoved them in there."

They opened the first box and began to go through its
contents. There were yearbooks and report cards, pictures and school papers. Many of the papers had comments written at the top. The remarks on Tanya's were
always glowing, while Sasha's teachers pleaded for her
to pay attention to what was going on in class, to try
harder and to stop daydreaming. And several of Sasha's
papers had drawings on them, but none of dolls.

For a while Jenny was content to investigate the room,
then she climbed up on the bed, next to her father, and
leafed through one of Sasha's yearbooks. Jenny did well
at entertaining herself, but by the time they'd gone
through the first box and were halfway through the second, she was restless. Teasingly she tickled her father
and, when he didn't respond, pulled a stack of papers out
of the box and ran for the door.

"Jennifer Marie Hammond, bring those back," ordered Ross.

"Please," Sasha added softly.

Sasha's mother laughed. "She reminds me of you,
Sasha. You were always looking for ways to gain attention."

Sasha watched Ross and waited, wondering how he
would handle the situation. Her father had been an ex-
pert at squelching her ploys for attention. His methods
were simple: berate or ignore. Neither response had been
what she'd wanted.

"Come on, girl, I know you're bored," Ross called to
his daughter. "Why don't you look through those papers and see if you can find any pictures of dolls."

Irena Peters had another idea. "Or how would you like
to go downstairs and help me make some no-bake cookies?"

Jenny cocked her head and studied the older woman but stayed where she was.

"Do you like peanut butter?" Irena asked.

With a vigorous nod Jenny made up her mind. The papers were dropped, Anna was collected, and Jenny went to Sasha's mother.

"Good choice. My mother makes the best no-bake cookies in the world," declared Sasha. She got up and walked over to retrieve the pile of papers.

"You don't mind?" asked Ross.

Grinning, Sasha's mother rumpled Jenny's mop of curls. "Not at all. Sasha always used to make no-bake cookies. It's been a while since I've had any. You two go on through those things. You know what you're looking for. I don't. Jenny and I will make the cookies, then I'll fix us some lunch."

Sasha sat down on the bed next to Ross and one by one she went through the papers Jenny had taken. Most were from her days in kindergarten and the first grade, and each brought back memories. Even in those early grades she'd drawn on her schoolwork, but none of the stick figures they saw could be called designs for a doll.

"What was it like living here?" Ross asked without warning.

"What was it like?" Sasha's gaze left the paper in her hand to meet with his.

"Did he physically abuse you?"

She looked back down at the page. "No."

"Maybe hit you harder than he should have?" Ross was certain her father had.

"No. Never. Dad never hit either of us." Flipping through the remaining papers, Sasha tried to act casually. "None of these has what we need. One more box to go."

She moved to open the last carton, but Ross caught her arm and stopped her. "Sasha, tell me about your father."

Again she looked at him. "I've already told you about him in your office. My father and I disagreed on a lot of things. He told me to leave home, and I did."

"And you're afraid of him." She'd said she was afraid of the bonds of marriage. He was beginning to understand why.

Sasha hesitated a moment, then nodded. "I guess I am."

"Did he sexually abuse you?" It was a possibility.

"No." She shook her head and glanced down at Ross's hand on her arm. He let her go, and she moved over to the box they hadn't yet looked through.

"Why are you afraid of him?" he asked softly.

For a moment Sasha stared at the unopened carton, then let her eyes return to Ross's face. "You've heard the old saying, 'Sticks and stones will break your bones, but words will never hurt you'? Well, believe me, words *can* hurt. Especially if you hear the same words over and over."

"What did he say to you?"

"That I was lazy, had no ambition and wasted my time. He used to say he wished I'd never been born. I think he meant it."

"And did he say these things to your sister?"

Sasha shook her head. "No. As far as he was concerned, Tanya was perfect. She did everything right, I did everything wrong."

"And what about your mother? What did she do?" He liked the woman he'd met and couldn't imagine her picking on Sasha or allowing her husband to.

"What could she do? Whenever she tried to stick up for me, Dad would yell at her. Actually he was always yelling at her. As far as he's concerned, Mom and I are alike—stupid and lazy—and Tanya's like him. But she's not, thank goodness. I mean, Tanya's not stupid or lazy, but she's not like Dad, either."

"You're not stupid or lazy, Sasha," insisted Ross, hating the man for even saying so. "And from the little I've seen of your mother, she isn't, either."

"I know that." She could hear her mother down in the kitchen, working. No, Irena Peters wasn't lazy. The house was always clean, meals were always ready on time and her father always went to work in a freshly laundered shirt. "I do think Mom's dumb for sticking with my father for thirty-one years. I keep telling her to leave him, that she could do better, but I know she never will. She's afraid she couldn't make it on her own." Sasha closed her eyes. "I can't imagine being trapped in a marriage like she is."

Once again Ross touched her, his fingers brushing lightly over her hand. "It doesn't have to be that way."

Her eyes opened and she stared at his face. She wanted to believe him. Then she looked back down at the box. "I think we'd better finish going through these papers."

"For now. But later we talk. Really talk."

THEY WERE A THIRD of the way through the box when they found the first sketch. Actually there were several drawings of dolls' heads on the back of a spelling list. Sasha had been experimenting with eye shapes. On the opposite side of the paper, in the upper left corner, was Sasha's name, the date and the grade. She'd been nine years old.

The next paper that had drawings that would help was only a few pieces down. The design of the doll had been worked out more thoroughly; the sketches showed the head with its realistic eyes, the navel, and how the stitching would have to be done to form the toes and fingers.

They never did find a drawing showing the dimples on the doll's bottom, but a note Sasha had written on the back of a fourth-grade long-division assignment mentioned the idea of using dimples. Ross was sure it would be enough. He had dates, grade levels and teachers' names to substantiate her priority in the design.

The final coup was their discovery of a copy of the elementary-school newspaper, published for and by the students. On the front page was an article written by Sasha on how to make a doll, including a description of the one she was working on.

"Eureka!" he cried, and waved the newspaper in front of her face. "This is all we need."

He did, however, suggest that they take all the drawings.

Ross was putting the three boxes back up on the shelf, with Sasha handing them to him, when she heard a sneeze, then the sound of a familiar deep male voice. "Irena, where are you?"

There was a moment of silence, then her mother's voice replied. "In the kitchen, Orrie."

Sasha froze and Ross quickly slid the last carton into place and pushed the linens in front of all three.

"Would you believe it? A simple cold and the boss tells me to go home."

Ross closed the closet door and turned to face Sasha. "What now?" he asked in almost a whisper.

"I don't know." Nervously she licked her lips. Her legs felt like rubber, and her insides had turned to gelatin.

"Who in the hell is this?"

Sasha knew her father had just seen Jenny and could imagine how the little girl felt when faced by the burly man with the cold blue eyes and booming voice. Instantly she knew what they had to do. She picked up the papers they needed and headed for the stairway. "Let's get down there quickly."

"Where'd she come from?" demanded Orrie Peters.

Her mother's answer didn't carry, but her father's response did. "She's here?"

As Sasha hurried down the hall, every muscle in her body was tense, her breathing shallow and her heart pounding. This was one scene she'd hoped to avoid.

The first thing she noticed was that ten years had turned her father's blond hair to gray, had added at least twenty pounds to his large frame and had increased the number of wrinkles on his face. But his cold blue eyes hadn't changed. At the threshold of the kitchen Sasha froze.

For a second he stared at her, his eyes narrowing as they moved from her face to the hem of her long skirt. His mouth was a taut, straight line when he looked back up. "So, you've come crawling home, have you?"

"I needed some papers," Sasha managed to say, the sound of her voice unusually high.

"Papers?"

"Drawings . . . of my dolls."

"Your dolls." He spat out the words, then looked past her. "And who's he?"

Ross had stopped behind her. Sasha glanced over her shoulder at him, then back at her father. "This is Ross Hammond, my lawyer. I think you've already met his daughter, Jenny."

Her father snorted. "Lawyer? So what kind of trouble you got yourself in, huh?"

"A man in New York says he designed the doll that Benson Toys bought from me."

"Probably did. I suppose you came running to Mama for money to try to prove he didn't." He looked at his

wife. "Don't you dare give her a cent. You hear me? I
don't put in long hours so this lazy no-good can squan-
der what I make."

"She didn't ask for money. She just wanted some old
school papers," her mother explained.

Orrie Peters glanced at the papers in Sasha's hand and
scowled. "I thought I told you to get rid of everything of
hers. What a pair you two make. Neither of you has the
brains to follow a simple order."

"Thank goodness your wife didn't follow your orders," Ross intervened.

"Oh yeah?" Sasha's father eyed him suspiciously.

"Yes. We found the drawings we need to prove Sasha's
case."

Sasha's mother smiled. Orrie Peters didn't. "Don't you
find it a little odd for a grown woman to be playing with
dolls?"

Ross's answer was simple. "No."

The older man shook his head. "Leave it to her to find
a lawyer as daft as she is."

Jenny climbed down from the chair Sasha's mother
had pushed next to the counter, picked up Anna and
grabbed a handful of cookies. She was headed for Ross
when Orrie Peters reached down and caught her by the
back of her shirt. Wide-eyed with fear, clutching doll and
cookies close to her chest, Jenny looked up at the burly
man.

"Don't you ask first before taking things?" he demanded.

Jenny looked at her father.

"Look at me, not him," Orrie Peters ordered, and Jenny's gaze met his. "Now, say 'May I have some cookies,
please?'"

"Dad, she can't talk."

He glanced at Sasha, then back down at Jenny. "What do you mean, she can't talk? Is the kid dumb?"

"Not dumb," both Ross and Sasha said at the same time. Ross stepped around Sasha and protectively moved toward his daughter. "She was in an accident and hasn't talked since. Let her go."

"Dumb woman picks lawyer with dumb kid. Double dumb," Orrie Peters mumbled to himself. He did let go of Jenny's arm.

Immediately Jenny went to Ross, and he picked her up.

Orrie Peters's eyes narrowed as his attention returned to Sasha. "I told you when you left home never to come back. I meant it. Now get out—all of you!"

"We're going," Sasha assured him. "Come on, Ross, let's go. Goodbye, Mom. Thanks for your help."

"Any time," she responded.

Her father's head snapped in her direction. "You know what I said before. You are not to see or talk to her. Now, go upstairs. I'll deal with you later."

"You touch a hair on her head, and I'll see you in court," warned Ross.

Anger flared in Orrie Peters's cold blue eyes, and he waved a finger at the door. "Get out of my house, or I'll have you arrested for trespassing."

"We'd better go. Dad won't hurt her," Sasha assured Ross. "He'll just rant and rave, as usual. Mom's used to it. We're both used to it. He likes cutting people down. Likes to make them feel like nothing." She noticed her mother hadn't moved.

And so did her father. "I said get upstairs," he repeated.

But her mother still didn't budge, and Sasha smiled. "Watch out, Dad, one of these days she's going to get tired of all your orders and put-downs, just as I did.

Someday she's going to walk out of this house and never
come back. And then where will you be?"

"Your mother's not going anywhere. Where would she
go? What would she do? Who would take in a middle-
aged woman who didn't even finish high school?"

"Don't underestimate Mom's abilities."

"Out!" her father repeated, and took a step toward her.
Ross tensed.

"Come on, Ross," Sasha urged. "For everyone's sake,
it would be better if we did leave. We have what we came
for."

A second passed before Ross moved. "We're going,"
he said, and looked toward Sasha's mother. "It was nice
meeting you. If you need any help, let us know."

"I'll be fine," Irena Peters answered.

She stayed behind in the kitchen, but Orrie Peters followed them to the front door and called out one last in-
sult as Sasha headed for Ross's car. "You look stupid in
that long dress. But then I suppose you'd want to cover
those legs. Tanya—"

"Tanya," Sasha muttered under her breath, not bothering to listen to what her father had to say about her
sister. All her life she'd been compared to Tanya.

Quickly Ross buckled Jenny in and got behind the
steering wheel. As soon as Sasha pulled her door closed,
he had the car started. A half block from her house, both
he and Sasha sighed in unison, glanced at each other,
then started laughing. It seemed the only way to ease the
tension.

"And that's the dragon," Sasha said when the laughter ended and her body felt limp.

"Well, we certainly didn't slay him," admitted Ross.
He hadn't known what to do. "Is he that way all the
time?"

"You mean loud and intimidating?"

"And always running you down?"

"Oh, once in a while he'd have a good word for me, but not often. I just never seemed to measure up to his expectations. No matter what I did, he didn't approve." She touched the skirt of her dress. "Like my clothes. He hated to see Tanya or me in shorts or pants—said a lady should look like a lady—but more often than not, he'd criticize my skirts and dresses."

"Well, I think you dress just fine—" he glanced her way and smiled "—other than I'd like to see a little more leg. He's wrong, you know. You've got great legs. Hungry?"

"In a way, Dad's right. When I was younger, I was always skinning my knees or getting bruises. My legs usually did look a mess. I'm starved."

"Good. Let's get some lunch, then take these papers over to Bernstein."

DURING LUNCH, SASHA opened up about her father. She told Ross about her childhood, about the long hours Orrie Peters had kept her in her room simply because she didn't do as well in school as her sister did, about his dislike of anything make-believe and about his old-fashioned ideas regarding a woman's position in a man's world. And the more she expressed her anger and frustration, the better she felt.

"You know, I think maybe it was a good thing that Dad came home and found us there. I'm glad I saw him again. I've remembered him as big and loud and very frightening. Today he was still big and loud, but he didn't scare me. In fact, standing there in the kitchen, listening to him bluster, I actually felt a little sorry for him."

"I didn't." There were few people Ross disliked on first meeting, but Orrie Peters was one. "He had Jenny scared to death."

"I know the feeling." She could laugh about it now.

"How can your mother stand it?"

Sasha had often wondered that herself. "I think Mom lacks the self-confidence to stand up to him. They were married when she was very young, and she came from an immigrant family where the father was the boss. If you think Dad's bad, you ought to have met my grandfather when he was alive."

Ross shook his head. He couldn't imagine a more chauvinistic, domineering, obnoxious man than her father. "Why did you get picked on and not Tanya?"

"Oh, Tanya didn't completely escape Dad's sharp tongue. Why do you think she moved so far away from them? Like me, she misses seeing Mom, but she hates the way Dad cuts everyone down. Things are always black-and-white to him. He's practical, goal oriented and pragmatic. And so's Tanya, to a point. My mother and I are the dreamers. We tend to live for today rather than tomorrow. And because we're not like him, Dad feels he has to straighten us out . . . lead us . . . control us. Mom usually complies with his orders, though I noticed she didn't today. I always fought his edicts."

Ross reached across the table and took her hand in his. "And won more often than you lost, I think."

"As a child I never felt I won." She gazed into the warm blue of Ross's eyes. It was good to have him know. "For eighteen years he tried to change me. I don't want to ever again have to fight for the right to be me."

"With me you won't have to," he assured her softly. "I like the Doll Lady just as she is."

AFTER LUNCH THEY DROVE across the Bay Bridge to San Francisco. First they had to convince Benjamin Bernstein's secretary that what they had was important enough to call the man out of a meeting. And when Bernstein opened his door, frowning, Sasha wondered if that had been such a good idea. But as soon as he saw the school newspaper with the description of Sasha's doll, the sketches and notes, her worries disappeared. Benjamin Bernstein was delighted. He canceled his meeting, called in his lawyers, had everything copied and assured Sasha that there would be no further problems. "Your check will be in the mail by the end of the week."

It was midafternoon by the time they left Benson Toys. Traffic was heavy and Ross said little as he drove across the Golden Gate Bridge and headed northeast. In the back seat of the car Jenny amused herself with the half-dozen toys Bernstein had given her. Exhausted from the events of the day, Sasha was asleep before they reached Sacramento.

They were on Highway 49, twisting their way up the mountainside, when she awoke. Foggily she tried to remember where she was and why. Turning her head toward Ross, she found him looking at her.

"Welcome back, sleepyhead."

Stifling a yawn, she stretched cramped muscles and sat forward. "How long was I asleep?"

"Quite a while. Won't be long and we'll be in Putnam. I think Jenny's asleep, too."

Sasha checked on the child. "She is. How about you? You must be exhausted. Want me to drive the rest of the way?"

"I think I can make it. I hate to stop and wake Jenny. She's been so good today." He leaned forward in his seat and flexed tired shoulders.

"When isn't Jenny good?" Reaching over, Sasha began to rub Ross's back and neck.

He chuckled. "You haven't seen one of her temper tantrums. She may not be able to talk, but she can sure stamp those feet. Hmm, that feels good."

The solid strength of his body felt good to her, too. He'd been by her side all day, understanding and supportive. For years she'd thought she wanted to stand alone; since meeting Ross, she'd discovered the pleasure of having someone to lean on.

Sasha pulled his shirt from his slacks, pushed it up a ways and massaged the small of his back. Ross gave a groan of pleasure.

"Remember the morning we walked on the beach, then went back to the hotel?" Her hands played around to his ribs. "I found out something about you that day."

Her fingers teased his sides, and he couldn't stop from wiggling. "Careful, or you'll have us over the edge."

Sasha glanced to the side. Beyond the guardrail there was a sharp drop to where the Yuba River flowed. She had no desire to see the river close up and brought her hands back to his shoulders.

"I found out something about you that day, too," he said, giving her a seductive smile.

"What could that be?" One last pat and she pulled his shirt down again, sat back in her seat and adopted a look of innocence.

"That you're one very sexy lady. How could such a perfect two days end so badly?" It was a question he'd asked himself over and over ever since.

"Maybe your companion needed to do some growing up?"

"I'm not like your father," he said, understanding.

"Some of the things you and your father said brought back painful memories."

He tried to remember what they'd said. "All I was trying to do was point out your options."

"It didn't sound like that—at least not to me. What I heard was you telling me I'd be a fool not to take Bernstein's offer, that I should think of the money, think of my future. Ross, that's what my father always used to say... that I was a fool to want to make dolls, that there was no money in it, that I should think of my future."

"Oh, Sasha. I never meant it that way. Never." Quickly he glanced her way. "Believe me, I was petrified you'd take the job. I didn't want you to, but I felt it had to be your choice."

She laughed ruefully. What a fool she'd been. Because she was oversensitive and afraid, she'd stayed away from this man for nearly two months, had repeatedly told herself she didn't need him. Well, she did need him. Being separated from Ross had been hell. Alone, she'd discovered, could be just that—very lonely.

"You know, I once told you my motto was 'Forget yesterday, live for today and hope for tomorrow.' I don't think I've been following my own advice." She hadn't forgotten her yesterdays; she'd allowed her father's cruel words and dictatorial attitude to cripple her. "I—"

"Oh, my God!"

She saw him tense. His foot went for the brake, and he swung the steering wheel radically to the right.

Thrown to the side, Sasha grabbed for a hold and looked out the windshield. What she saw made her suck in her breath. Only a few yards away a car was coming directly toward them. Next to it was the car it was passing.

"Oh, no!" She gasped and tightened her hold. There wasn't room on the pavement for three cars.

Ross was trying to get onto the shoulder, but there wasn't much of a shoulder to get onto, and the granite slope on the other side of the road limited that car's maneuverability. The BMW's outside tires hit gravel, and the car bounced and jerked. To her right, all Sasha could see was empty space. "Ross!" she cried. With her heart in her throat, she squeezed her eyes shut and waited for the moment they would hit the guardrail.

All she could think about were the rocks below. *It's not the fall that kills you, it's the landing* flashed through her mind.

She wasn't ready to die. Who would take care of Nero and Polo, the cat and the goat? She had the doll order for the hospital to complete. She wanted to have babies. Lots of babies. Ross's babies.

The car gave a lurch to the left, the crunch of gravel gave way to the hum of pavement, and Sasha's eyes snapped open. It was over. They were safe. Alive. The danger had passed. The two oncoming cars had gone by, Ross had managed to keep the BMW on the road and the highway ahead was clear.

Ross slowed down. His knuckles were white, his eyes directed straight ahead, his mouth a tight line. Taking in a deep breath, he eased over to the shoulder again. Turning off the engine, he slumped back against the seat, closed his eyes and exhaled. "That was close."

"I thought for sure we were going to go over," Sasha admitted shakily. She, too, let herself relax. Her muscles suddenly went very limp, and a strong urge to cry took control. Tears streaming down her cheeks, she looked back at Jenny.

The child's face was pale, her eyes wide with fear. "Come here," urged Sasha, and Jenny quickly released her seat belt and crawled between the two seats to reach Sasha's lap.

"Were you scared?" asked Sasha.

Jenny nodded, tears filling her blue eyes and silently spilling onto her cheeks. Sasha cuddled her close, and Ross reached over to rub his daughter's small arms. "That idiot should be hung by his thumbs. That section of the road's marked No Passing. He could have killed us all in his hurry to get wherever he's going."

"I don't see how you maintained control." Sasha's entire body was shaking now. She started laughing and the tears rolled down her cheeks. "I think I'm going to have hysterics."

Ross slipped his arms around her neck, enfolding both woman and child in his embrace. His emotions weren't any too steady, either. Thinking back, he didn't really know what he'd done to keep from hitting the car in his lane or from going over the edge. Every move had been pure instinct, a basic act of survival. As the reality of how close they'd come to death dawned on him, he could feel tears filling his own eyes. One hand dropped to caress Jenny's head; his other massaged Sasha's neck. He could have lost both of them. The two most important people in his life—and some crazy driver had almost taken them from him.

A car passed them going up the grade. Then another. Slowly Ross's heartbeat returned to normal, and the shaking of his legs disappeared. He looked at Sasha, and she smiled at him. Her tears were gone, but her eyes glistened. He smiled back, straightened, and started the car.

FOR THE REST of the trip Jenny stayed on Sasha's lap. Sasha cuddled the child close, and Ross kept up a dialogue as he drove, reaching over every few minutes to touch them, as though reassuring himself that they were there and all right. Verbally he criticized every careless driver in the state, then took on the Department of Motor Vehicles, the highway system and road engineers. Sasha knew he was still upset and needed to let it out.

But by the time they pulled into her yard, even Ross had grown quiet. As soon as he turned off the car's engine, Jenny was pulling on the door handle, trying to get out, and the two dogs were jumping on the side of the car, trying to get in. "Nero! Polo! Down!" Sasha ordered.

They ignored her until she opened the door, and Jenny scrambled out. Immediately the two dogs began licking the child's face.

Ross got out and came around to Sasha's side. "I'm a little concerned about her," he said, watching his daughter dash over to the fence to greet the goat, the dogs following. "All of the psychiatrists we've seen feel Jenny doesn't talk because of the trauma of being trapped in the car with her dead mother. We've been trying to get her to accept what happened. I sure hope today's incident doesn't set her back."

"I hope not, either." Sasha also watched Jenny. The little girl didn't look upset. She was busy pulling weeds to feed the goat. "She seems happy to be here. Want to stay for a while?"

Ross reached over and brushed his fingers through Sasha's pale blond curls. His gaze moved from her eyes to her lips. "How long is a while?"

"Maybe the night?" She'd made up her mind. The past would be forgotten. "I finished that other bedroom. There's a bed for Jenny."

"Sounds good to me." Weeks of separation and to-day's near accident had left him willing to accept whatever terms she offered.

"I've got to milk the goat and feed the animals, then I'll fix us some dinner." She wasn't sure what she had in the refrigerator, but they could always have soup and sandwiches.

"Why don't you let me pick up a pizza?"

That sounded better than soup and sandwiches. When Ross called to Jenny, she didn't want to go. "Leave her here. She can help me milk the goat," Sasha suggested, and Ross agreed.

Jenny did come running when Ross started the car, but as soon as Sasha explained that he'd be back and that they were going to milk the goat, the little girl grinned and dashed off to get the bucket.

It took Sasha almost an hour—with Jenny's help—to milk the goat and feed the animals. When she finished, she left Jenny in the living room to play with the dolls and went to her bedroom. A quick shower washed off the grime of the day, then she slipped on clean underwear. She looked through the long dresses in her closet, reached for a flowered cotton, then changed her mind. In the bottom drawer of her dresser she found what she wanted.

In a neat pile were three pairs of shorts. She'd saved them for years, though until this moment she'd never known why. She pulled on a navy pair. A flowered cotton blouse and white sandals completed her outfit. Standing in front of the bathroom's full-length mirror, she studied her image. It had been a long time since she'd worn anything but her Victorian-style dresses. A slow turn gave her a view of her backside. It was rather nice seeing her legs again. They really weren't that bad looking. Not bad at all.

The dogs' barking announced Ross's return. Jenny was out the door and to the car before Sasha stepped outside. The child hugged and kissed her father, then crawled over the seat to the back to get her precious Anna and the toys Bernstein had given her. Ross lifted a pizza box off the front passenger seat, stacked a six-pack of beer and a six-pack of Coke on top and straightened. He waited until Jenny got out of the car with all her treasures before he pushed the door closed with his hip. The little girl headed straight for the house. Turning in that direction, Ross saw Sasha.

She smiled at his astonished expression. His eyes raked over her, coming to rest on the curves of her legs. His grin told her he was pleased with what he saw. "What a nice surprise," he said as he walked toward her.

"It's so warm, shorts seemed in order." She tried to make it sound like a casual decision. They both knew it was more than that.

He'd stopped at his house while he was gone. His white slacks and striped shirt had been replaced by well-worn jeans, a beige T-shirt and tennis shoes, and she had a feeling he'd taken a shower. His hair was rumpled, as though he hadn't taken the time to dry it. "Ready to eat?" he asked, the aroma of pizza preceding his advance.

"Starved." It had been hours since they'd had lunch.

"Me, too." He stopped beside her and leaned close to kiss her lips.

He'd meant it to be just a quick kiss, but she tasted too good to leave. "So hungry," he murmured as he went back for another kiss. "Famished," he uttered sincerely, his mouth taking hers for a third time, then a fourth.

His kisses were becoming more ardent, and if his hands hadn't been occupied with a pizza and two six-packs, he would have taken her in his arms. But his hands were full, and a pull on his leg reminded him they weren't alone. Straightening, he looked down at Jenny. As usual, she was gesturing. First she pointed to the pizza box, then to the house. Her meaning was clear.

"How's she been?" he asked as Sasha walked with him into the house.

"Fine as far as I can tell. Full of energy. Don't yell at her for the mess with the dolls. I'll get her to clean it up later."

"I won't yell at her." He now understood Sasha's sensitivity. "But I know one thing—" his eyes drifted down over her body, and he grinned wickedly "—Jenny's going to bed as soon as she's had dinner."

THOSE WERE ROSS'S plans, not Jenny's. Her nap in the car, the scare of their near accident and the toys Bernstein had given her all acted as stimulants. Without saying a word she talked Sasha into telling a story. And hugs and kisses got her father to do a puzzle with her. It was after ten o'clock before Ross was able to get her into the nightgown he'd brought back with him. She bounced on the bed Sasha had bought at a yard sale, climbed off to find Anna, bounced on the bed again, hugged Sasha and Ross three times each, then gestured that she needed a drink of water. Finally, at ten thirty-seven, she fell asleep.

"I don't believe her," Ross grumbled as they left the room. "Normally she's asleep by eight."

"She knows what wicked thoughts I have in mind, and she's trying to protect her poor father," Sasha explained.

"Wicked thoughts?" Ross stopped and put a hand on Sasha's arm to stop her, too. Eyebrows raised, he looked at her, then smiled. "How wicked?"

"How wicked do you want them to be?"

"Very." He wrapped his arms around her and drew her close, bringing her breasts to his chest. "Because you know what I want to do?"

"What?"

"I want to tear off all your clothes, sling you over my shoulder and carry you off to the bedroom." The thought created an immediate reaction in his body, and he felt his jeans tighten.

Looking into his eyes, Sasha watched his pupils dilate and his irises darken. His hands began to move over her back. Slowly. Sensuously. "And when you get me into the bedroom?" she asked, her own voice husky.

"I'll make love to you. All night long. Every way I know. Any way you'd like." His mouth found hers and he stopped talking. Words couldn't express his desire.

His lips, however, did a very good job. His tongue pressed into her mouth, and she held it there, played with it, then released it. Deep inside she felt a tension growing, an emptiness he could fill. He moved a leg between hers, and she rubbed against it slowly, the pressure bringing her pleasure. His mouth left hers to plant kisses on her cheeks and forehead. His breathing was no longer even and his words were a hoarse plea. "Oh, Sasha, I want you."

"And I want you." She had already pulled the hem of his T-shirt free from the waistband of his jeans. Her hands moved up under the soft cotton to rub over his back. His skin felt smooth and warm.

He didn't sling her over his shoulder but did lift her into his arms. Easily he carried her to her bedroom, snapping on the light and closing the door behind him. Placing Sasha on the bed, he stretched out beside her. "Now for the clothes."

"Right," she agreed and pulled his T-shirt up and over his head. Eyeing his chest, she ran her fingers through the springy curls that spread from his collarbone to just below his nipples. From there the hairs formed a narrow line that disappeared beneath his waistband. Her hands moved to that point, and she unsnapped his jeans. "You really have too many clothes on."

He chuckled but didn't disagree. Carefully she pulled down the zipper, exposing a pair of navy briefs that bulged in front. Her knuckles rubbed over the rise in the material, and she heard Ross take in a quick breath. Again he chuckled, and she knew he was enjoying every minute.

She had to sit up and take off his tennis shoes and socks before she could strip the denims from his legs. That accomplished, she took a moment to simply enjoy the way he looked with only the blue briefs covering his body. "Sexy." It was all she could think of to say.

Reaching out, she ran a fingernail lightly over his leg, starting just above his kneecap and moving up, over his hip to his ribs. She felt him twitch and glanced up at his face to find him watching her, smiling. "Minx."

"Me?" she asked in mock innocence. "Now, can I help it if my hands slip and you're ticklish?"

She ran her hands over his chest, crossing the rigid nubs of his flat breasts. Man and woman. They were so different. Her fingers moved down toward the dark blue cotton briefs that contrasted with the tan of his skin. She could see the definite outline of the one part of his body that was undeniably different from hers. Like a magnet it drew her hand to it, and as she caressed him, she heard Ross groan in pleasure, saw his smile and the glow of passion in his hooded eyes.

She knew without question that she loved this man and wanted to spend the rest of her life with him. Perhaps she'd never truly forget the pain of her childhood, but the past no longer ruled her life.

"Touch me more," Ross said softly, and she understood his need and stripped the briefs from his hips. He wiggled free of them and kicked them off the edge of the bed.

He was a contrast of soft and hard, baby smooth and manly rigid. One place his skin was cool, another hot. Her fingers caressed, explored and teased. And as she brought him to the height of desire, her actions stimulated her own body. Her bra felt too tight for her swollen breasts, her nipples hard against the nylon. Between her legs there was an ache she knew Ross could satisfy.

When he began to unbutton her blouse, she helped him. Then she turned so he could release the clasp of her bra. As soon as he'd freed her breasts from their confines, he touched them, rubbing and caressing, then bringing her down toward him so he could pull a nipple into his mouth. "And God made woman," he murmured, switching to the other breast.

It was a while before he spoke again. Lying back, letting his hands drift to her shorts, he grinned up at Sasha. "He did a wonderful job when He made you."

She slipped out of her shorts, underpants and sandals. Ross switched positions with her, placing her flat on the bed, spreading her legs and positioning himself between them. Sitting back on his heels, he brought her legs close to his hips and began to rub her calf muscles. Softly, his voice barely above a whisper, he spoke to her, telling her how much she pleased him, how much he cared.

The gentle kneading pressure of his hands was both relaxing and stimulating, and Sasha could feel other muscles tighten in anticipation. When his fingers moved up to her thighs, she was ready, open to his lambent gaze and eager for his touch.

Finally it came. Lightly, feathery at first, a little tentative until he heard her sigh in relief and saw her smile. Then his fingers grew bolder, the rhythm of his strokes increasing until her body arched beneath his hand, and he knew she was close.

Too close. "Ross, please," she begged, stopping him. "I don't want to come this way, I want you inside me, filling me."

He had no objections. Carefully he settled himself over her.

A deep sense of completeness washed over her as he entered her. Two had become one. Their differences matched, enhanced and satisfied. He moved within her, searching for the right spot to give her the ultimate satisfaction. He paused to kiss her lips and tell her of his love, then he began the rhythm again.

Every touch, every kiss, every whispered word gave her pleasure. Different positions introduced new feelings, all steadily building to a heightened level of passion. And then the moment came, and her body surrendered. Ross held her close, and the throbbing sweetness was hers to enjoy completely.

She had no idea how much time passed before he spoke. "You okay?"

"Fine," she answered, then the laughter bubbled out. "Simply mahvelous."

He chuckled at her response and captured her lips. Deeply he drank in her kiss before he began to move his hips again. In his search for his own release, the bed rocked under his driving thrusts, his body grew hot, his breathing labored. Sasha wrapped her arms around his damp shoulders and arched her back.

"Yes, yes," he cried, then his body stilled. After a long time spent planting kisses on her face and neck, he rolled to her side.

Gently he drew her to him so that their bodies touched. His sexual need had been satisfied, but he still wanted her close. "With you I feel complete," he murmured into her ear.

"I know what you mean." For two months they'd been apart. The tears, the restless, empty feelings—she'd blamed them on all the wrong things.

"I do love you." He hoped she knew that. "I can't promise—"

His words were cut off by a sudden cry from the other room. "Jenny!" he gasped, sitting up even as he said his daughter's name.

Sasha also sat up. The sound from the child had been one of terror.

Quickly Ross grabbed his jeans from the floor, hopped on one foot as he stuck the other into a pant leg. By the time he reached the door, he had both legs in. He pulled the zipper up as he left the room.

Sasha grabbed for her shorts and blouse, forgetting underwear. Jenny's pathetic cries continued, the sound tearing at Sasha's heart. She followed Ross to the other room, then stopped in the doorway. He was already at the bed, lifting Jenny into his arms. Sitting at the edge of the mattress, he cradled her, rocking her back and forth, soothing her.

"Mama," Jenny cried. "Mama. Mama." Over and over, she repeated the word, her little body shaking.

12

"MAMA'S GONE, HONEY, but I'm here," Ross gently consoled her. "I'm here and I love you."

Slowly Jenny's sobs lessened, she hiccuped and sniffed. Then, reaching up with her small hand, she touched Ross's chin. "I love you, too, Daddy."

Sasha could feel the tears streaming down her cheeks and didn't care. She could see tears on Ross's cheeks and knew he didn't care. He cuddled Jenny close, talking to her all the time, the words coming straight from his heart.

"I've missed hearing you talk, honey. Missed it so much. Once, long ago, I told you to be quiet, that I didn't want to hear another word out of you, but I didn't mean it. I didn't realize then how beautiful your voice is. I didn't know how much I'd miss hearing it. Please, don't ever stop talking again."

"Don't cry, Daddy," Jenny said, her fingers wiping away the tears on his cheek. "I'll talk."

He laughed in relief, and still holding Jenny close, rubbed his forearm across his face. Only then did he look toward Sasha. Laughing like a kid who'd just discovered soap bubbles, he proudly announced, "She can talk."

"So I hear." Sasha had to wipe away her own tears, and her eyes shimmered as she made her way to the two on the bed.

"I love you, too, Sasha," Jenny said with a slight lisp, and, twisting toward Sasha, held out her arms.

Ross transferred his daughter to Sasha and again wiped at his eyes.

"And I love Anna. And Nero. And Polo. And the goat. And the cat."

Both Ross and Sasha laughed as the list went on.

"And Mama." Jenny's tone changed, a sadness in her voice beyond her years. Pressing her head against Sasha's breasts, she sniffed and grew quiet. "I miss Mama."

"I know," said Sasha, rubbing a hand over Jenny's back.

"I didn't want to go with that man. I told Mama I didn't want to go."

Jenny was crying, and Ross touched her. "You don't have to talk about it, honey."

But nothing would stop her now. "He yelled at me. I said I didn't wanna go, and he told me to shut up." Jenny hiccuped and pressed her face closer to Sasha. "And then I was on the floor and I hurt and I couldn't talk and Mama wouldn't talk to me. Mama . . ."

"Don't cry, baby," Ross crooned.

"Maybe she needs to," suggested Sasha. "Maybe we all need to wash away the past."

For a while Jenny's sobs filled the room. Then they stopped and she was quiet. Frightened by her silence, Ross touched her shoulder. "Jenny, talk to me."

She turned her head to look at him, blinked away the last of her tears and smiled. "About what?"

He sighed in relief. "About anything."

"Can we live here? I like being with Sasha better than Man'y. Man'y's bossy."

Self-consciously Ross laughed and looked at Sasha. "That's up to Sasha."

"I'd like to have you move in here with me, but what about your place?"

"No problem." He wasn't going to let a little thing like a house keep him from Sasha. "I could keep my office there. Maybe rent out the house or keep it available for when my folks or yours come for a visit."

Sasha laughed. "Don't expect *my* folks to come up here to visit me."

"Even for our wedding?" He held his breath, unsure what her response would be.

"I'm quite sure this is one bride who won't be given away by her father."

Ross's sigh of relief was audible, his grin contagious. "I take it that means you'll marry me?"

"It's one way to get out of paying my lawyer's bill." She laughed again, then grew serious. "No, I don't really mean that. Just as soon as I get the money from Benson Toys, I want to pay that bill and give you back the money you loaned me. I want us to start out as equals. I don't want to owe you anything."

Ross reached over, took her hand in his and gave it a gentle squeeze. "If anyone owes anyone anything, it's me. You've made Jenny happy and taught me what love really means. I want to spend my whole life repaying you."

"One thing I'm sure you realize by now—I won't take having you yell at me," she warned. "And I won't let you yell at or berate Jenny. . . or any of our children."

The idea that she wanted children—his children—pleased him. "If I start yelling, tell me to go soak my head."

"I will."

He was sure she would. "So when are we getting married?"

"That's up to Jenny." Sasha tenderly brushed a hand over Jenny's matted curls. "How would you feel if I married your daddy?"

"Would you be my mama then? Would I call you Mama?" Jenny asked seriously.

"I know I can't take your mother's place. You can just call me Sasha, if you'd like."

Jenny thought about that.

"So, what do you think?" asked Ross, concerned. "Is it all right if I marry Sasha?"

"Sure," Jenny said casually.

Sasha was relieved. "And would you be in our wedding? Will you be our flower girl?"

"Can Anna be a flower girl, too?"

"I'd love to have Anna be one of the flower girls."

"But not Man'y. I don't want Man'y to be a flower girl."

Ross shook his head. "And I thought you two were getting along so well."

Jenny yawned, her eyes growing heavy. "Man'y's okay. Just talks too much."

They put Jenny back under the covers and stood by the bed until they thought she was asleep. She called out to them, however, before they left the room. "Night, Daddy. Night, Sasha."

Sasha glanced at Ross and smiled.

IRENA PETERS STOOD in the front pew and looked toward the back of the little mountain-town church. Coming up the aisle was Jenny, wearing a pink Victorian-style floor-length dress and carrying a basket of pink rose petals...and her doll, dressed identically to her. As she took each slow, carefully practiced step to the music, Jenny grinned at the people watching her and scattered a few of the rose petals over the white runner....

For the past twenty-four hours Jenny had been entertaining Irena. From the moment she'd stepped out of her car in front of Sasha's house, Irena had been bombarded with questions from the child. Was "the mean man" with her? Why didn't he come? Why didn't he want to see Sasha? Was she going to be in the wedding? Why not? Would she stay? Where would she sleep?

She'd been glad to see Sasha come out of the house.

"Mom, what a surprise." Sasha had found it hard to believe her eyes.

"I decided to come." Not that it had been an easy decision. "Your father, of course, ordered me not to." Irena Peters smiled. "To say the least, he was dumfounded when I told him he could pretend he didn't have a second daughter if he wanted to, but I wasn't going to."

"Jenny, go see if you can find those new baby kittens. We'll show them to Nana," Sasha suggested, sending Jenny off. She wanted to hear what her mother had to say—uninterrupted. "And what was Dad's response?"

"He blustered, ranted, tried not talking to me, then—yesterday—told me I'd better be back right after the wedding or not come home at all. Not that I will. Go back right after the wedding, that is. I figured I'd spend today and tomorrow before the wedding helping you, then tomorrow night and the next day with Tanya. That is, if you don't mind."

"Mind? I'm delighted—" Sasha hugged her mother "—shocked, surprised, but absolutely delighted."

Irena chuckled and hugged her daughter back. "I think your father was also shocked. But lately I have been shocking him quite regularly by refusing to jump at his commands. About three months ago I went to the doctor's because I'd been having bad headaches, my stomach was bothering me and I was feeling depressed. Dr. Delf's diagnosis was that I was suffering from an overbearing, ill-tempered husband. He knows your dad. Anyway, he said if I didn't want to end up in a hospital bed, I'd better either leave your father or learn to handle him so I wasn't under so much stress."

"I've often wondered why you haven't left him," Sasha admitted. Stepping back, she took her mother's arm. "Come on inside. Tell me more."

Irena walked with her daughter into the house. "There's not a lot to tell. The most important thing is I've joined a support group that meets at the hospital once a week. Listening to others who are in situations like mine, talking about my problems, I'm beginning to understand why I never stood up to your father."

"Why didn't you?" Sasha had never understood.

They both sat down on the sofa, and Irena took her daughter's hand in hers. "In part because—as overbearing as he could be—your father was simply trying to make life better for me and you girls. You don't know how difficult it was during World War II, when we had to scrimp and save. And neither of us had come from wealthy, well-educated families. We wanted an easier life for you. We wanted both you and Tanya to do well in school, for you both to go on to college. Tanya was no problem. You . . ." Her mother sighed, remembering.

"I didn't interfere when your dad made you stay in your room and study because I knew I'd used my low grades as an excuse to drop out of high school. And I thought maybe his yelling at you might make you realize how important money is."

Again she sighed. Her gaze locked with Sasha's, she shook her head. "No, those were the excuses I gave myself for too many years. In our group we're learning to get at the truth. And the truth is, the reason I never stood up to your father is I'm a coward. Or at least *was* a coward. I was afraid of him. Afraid he'd yell at me. Scared to death he'd leave me."

Her mother's head drooped and the tears started. Sliding an arm around the older woman's shoulders, Sasha gave her a hug. "It's all right, Mom. I understand."

"How you turned out to be such a talented, well-adjusted woman, I don't know," she replied, sniffling.

"The talent I inherited from you and Dad. It took Ross to make me well adjusted," Sasha admitted, finding a tissue in her pocket and handing it to her mother. "I've come to terms with my feelings toward Dad. It sounds like you're doing the same. Do you think you'll leave him?"

Irena sniffed, wiped at her nose and raised her head to look at her daughter. "I really don't know. Crazy as it may sound, I do love him. And I believe in the commitment of marriage. I don't expect miracles, but if he can change a little, stop yelling at me, start respecting me as an equal, maybe we can work it out. If not . . ."

"You'll always be welcome here," Sasha said softly. Her mother could live in Ross's house. It would be nice to have her nearby.

"Thank you." Blinking her eyes dry, Irena smiled. "So, tell me about you. When I talked to Tanya, she said your dolls would be in the stores before Christmas and something about a medical doll."

"I'm making some for a local hospital. Ross thinks I should patent the idea, believes I could sell it, too. Not that it would make as much money as the Friends dolls. I don't know, though. We'll see. I like the idea of making the dolls, but with what I've gotten from Benson Toys, I really don't need to worry about making a lot of money. Ross has enough for us to live comfortably for the rest of our lives." It felt nice to be in a financially secure position. "I think I'm simply going to enjoy being a wife to Ross and a mother to Jenny. Not that I'll completely give up doll making. And this winter I'll probably hold my story hour."

"Nana, look!" Jenny called, coming into the house carrying a tiny kitten....

The organist began the "Wedding March," and Irena's thoughts snapped back to the present. Ross's sister, Ann, had followed Jenny down the aisle. And behind her had come Tanya. Now Sasha stepped into view.

Irena didn't try to stop the tears when she saw her daughter. Dressed in white batiste trimmed with lace and carrying a bouquet of pink and white rosebuds, Sasha looked more beautiful than ever. A lacy veil capped her pale blond curls but exposed her face. Her shining green eyes were directed just to the right of the pulpit, toward Ross; her rose-colored lips formed a smile.

Bruce was giving her away and looked proud of the honor. Sasha rested her arm on his and took slow steps. Her gaze drifted to the front pew and she smiled.

Irena smiled back.

At the end of the aisle Bruce paused, and Sasha stepped forward. Two steps took her to Ross's side.

The first time she'd met him, Irena had thought Ross quite good-looking; in a tuxedo, he was devastatingly handsome. She couldn't have wished for a better match for her daughter; the man loved and honored Sasha in a way no words or official paper could duplicate.

The ceremony was a short one. As Ross kissed his new bride, Irena felt more tears slide down her cheeks and smiled. A bride's mother was supposed to cry at the wedding. She was doing her job well.

"Ready to go to the reception, Nana?" a small voice asked by her side.

Looking down, Irena saw Jenny, still carrying her doll and the basket, with only a few rose petals remaining. The child held out her free hand.

"Ready," Irena answered, and took Jenny's fingers in hers.

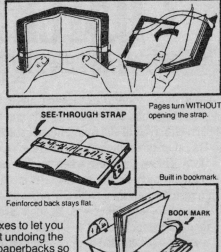

Janet DAILEY

THE MASTER FIDDLER

Jacqui didn't want to go back to college, and she didn't want to go home. Tombstone, Arizona, wasn't in her plans, either, until she found herself stuck there en route to L.A. after ramming her car into rancher Choya Barnett's Jeep. Things got worse when she lost her wallet and couldn't pay for the repairs. The mechanic wasn't interested when she practically propositioned him to get her car back—but Choya was. He took care of her bills and then waited for the debt to be paid with the only thing Jacqui had to offer—her virtue.

Watch for this bestselling Janet Dailey favorite, coming in June from Harlequin.

Also watch for *Something Extra* in August and *Sweet Promise* in October.